Sins

of the

Father

Sins of the Father

Smokey Moment

A
Smokey Moment
Novel

Sins of the Father

Smokey Moment

This book is fiction based on the imagination of the writer. Names, characters, places, and incidents are creations of the writer for entertainment purposes only. Any resemblance to actual people, living or deceased, is purely coincidental.

Sins of the Father

Smokey Moment

Become a Social Media Friend. Follow me on:

Twitter: smokeymomentbo1

Instagram: smokey.moment

Facebook: smokeymomentbooks

OR

Visit my website:

http://www.smokeymomentbooks.com

Sins of the Father

Smokey Moment

Join Our Newsletter

Text SMOKEY to 66866 to stay notified of new releases, character reveals, cover reveals, freebies and other exciting book stuff!

Free eBook Novella!

Smokey Moment

Join the most exciting newsletter! Visit my website to sign up and enjoy all the perks. Promotional offers, chapter snippets, cover reveals, freebies and so much more!

www.smokeymomentbooks.com

Worry free sign up. We do not share, sell or spam our readers email in boxes. You are in good hands. You will only hear from us when there is something exciting to share!

Smokey Moment

Smokey Moment

Acknowledgments

Was in my feelings with this one. I write what I feel, which for me, is the only way to write a story a person can connect to. Thank you to all that cheer each new release. I couldn't possibly be doing this without your support.

XOXO

Smokey Moment

Table of Contents

Smokey Moment

Trigger Warning

Reader discretion is advised.

Smokey Moment

Chapter One

A New Start

"Hey now…None of that. She's not going away forever. Why the tears," Rohan said, as he walked up to his wife and gave her a firm hug. He rocked side to side, as he held her snug, trying to calm his overly anxious wife. Monica was the glue. The rock. Her loving spirit and gift for making things better served him and his girls well.

But this was not a good day for the normally solid and put together woman. Her heart was heavy. Her eighteen year old, straight-A student daughter, was going off to college in Michigan and she was beside herself. Even though they were in Ohio, it would still feel far. She might as well be headed to a school in California. Just two days prior, it was Rohan who was eerily quiet, walking around like he'd lost his best friend. Now he stood comforting her as they prepared to take the hour and twenty minute drive to Ann Arbor to drop Avery off at her college dorm. Avery had a room mate that they were anxious to meet as well.

Meeting the young lady was just as important as anything. The Jeffries girls were brought up in a Christian household with strict parents who closely monitored everything including their daughter's friendships. If the friends did not meet the family's approval, the girls would be persuaded to find other friends. As each daughter grew older, more freedoms were allowed. But Rohan and Monica continued to keep their still, watchful eyes, on them.

They were, after all, the daughters of a well-known and popular congressman and their behaviors were a reflection of the entire family. Rohan and Monica didn't particularly want to invade their daughters lives, but it was imperative that the girls show restraint and character when it came to the difficult parts of life.

"You ready sweetheart?" Monica said, as she entered her daughter spacious bedroom. Their six bedroom, four bath, seven thousand square foot home was spectacular in every way. From the plush gardens to the lavish furniture, it was all a statement meant to show the world that the son of an immigrant from Jamaica had conquered the American dream. Rohan was as handsome and sophisticated as he was worldly. His dark captivating eyes drew in almost everyone who met him. There wasn't one person who could say a negative thing about him except that he carried with him all the attributes that made other men envious.

"I'm almost ready mom," Avery said, as she looked around her room then walked over to her bed and zipped her bright pink carryall closed.

"We should get going before the after-work traffic makes the drive impossible," Rohan warned.

Avery looked at her father and nodded. He gave her a half smile then turned from the doorway. Monica appreciated her husband's drive. He was always thinking. Always aware of the what-ifs. His brain worked like a 24 hour think tank, always checking this and that in order to make their lives easier. Monica sometimes forgot to have a say in most matters. She was so used to Rohan taking the lead, that she just chilled and followed. She trusted in his judgement. He was a family man who put her and her girls above all others.

The Jeffries drove in silence towards Ann Arbor Michigan. Rohan checked on Avery throughout the drive, glancing in his rear-view mirror and giving her a smile whenever she got the nerve to look. He was making her more nervous. Going off alone was bad enough without him making her feel like a kid being dropped off at daycare.

But Avery Jeffries was starting her life as a college student. Her parents were the power couple Monica and Congressman Rohan Jeffries. She had pride in the name but planned to not use it for benefit. Avery wanted pure friends. Real people who valued her. She didn't chase society approval. That was her father's job.

The family had made this run before. Avery was not the first Jeffries daughter to go off to college. Janine, Roxanne and Calista all went to college and were productive members of society. All except Calista. Despite being the most educated and holding the most esteemed degree, Calista chose to sit it out and take life one day at a time. Janine and Roxane, the two eldest, were self-sufficient, high earning career women. Monica and Rohan were proud.

Two out of four was not bad odds especially when a third was on her way to U of M Ann Arbor. Each girl held high degrees in challenging and rewarding fields and Avery felt the pressure. She wasn't sure she would fare as well. She believed her sisters were all smarter than her. She was the youngest and maybe the dumbest. Her mind played comparison games that pit her against them and it seemed she was never the victor. She had only one thing on them. The love of her father.

She was certain her father loved her the most. He doted on her the hardest and he did more for her than the others. Avery was proud of that fact. It kept her feeling superior in some way. But now she felt bare. She felt vulnerable. Without her witty and super intelligent father overseeing her every move, she wasn't sure she would prevail.

"We're here," Rohan said, putting the car in park and looking back at Avery. "What's that young lady's name?" he asked.

“Sophie. No wait…It’s Sophie,” Avery replied.

“Have you talked to her?” he asked.

“No dad. The college just informed me of what her name was. I haven’t met her yet.”

“You didn’t look her up on Facebook or anything?”

Avery rolled her eyes. He was ready to pick apart the young lady before they even laid eyes on her.

“No! I want to meet her first. I’m sure she’s a nice girl,” Avery said.

“Of course she is sweetie. And if not, we will get the college to reassign you to another room,” her mother Monica interjected.

“The rooms are full. I was told they always fill up until maybe second or third semester when some of the students drop out or move to a different school,” Avery said, looking around at the dense shrubs and trees that surrounded the dorm.

“No, no. That rule applies for everyone else. If this roommate does not work out for you, then you will be moved.

One phone call from your father and it will be done. Don't forget… you're the daughter of a congressman," Monica said proudly.

"How could I ever forget mom. You're always reminding me."

"Avery! Watch your mouth," Monica said.

"Now dear. She's just nervous. She didn't mean a word of it. Aint that right sweetheart?" Rohan said.

"Yes, daddy!"

The Jeffries got out of their black and silver Maybach and waited for Rohan to pop the trunk. Avery kept her eyes focused on the young men and women who came and went. A group of girls whispered then smile at Avery after checking over her father. It was the same reaction she always got. Rohan with his chiseled features, grey hair and goatee and fit physique always drew whispers and smiles. He looked like Hollywood royalty. So did Monica. Avery was over it.

A knock on the door went unanswered as the family waited. A muffled laugh erupted from inside that sounded far away. Avery knocked again as her parents stood, hand in hand, looking like a snapshot of a couple from a Harlequin romance novel.

“This is not good. Terrible first impression,” Rohan said.

“Shh dear. They might hear you. Knock again sweetheart,” Monica said. Avery knocked harder and soon the sound of approaching foot steps drew close.

“Hello,” the young woman answered.

“Hi…I’m Avery Jeffries,” she said.

“Oh…My roommate. Sorry about that. Come on in,” the woman said. Avery walked in as her parents followed close behind.

“Sorry for the mess. I guess I packed a little too much. My mother said I would be home sick if I didn’t bring all the things that make me, me. So… I brought everything except my bedroom set. It worked. I don’t feel homesick. Not yet anyways… I’m Sophie.”

“Nice to meet you. These are my parents. My mom Monica and my Father Rohan.”

"Rohan Jefferies. Wow! I am rooming with the daughter of the great Rohan Jefferies."

"You know my work?" he asked.

"Of course I do. My major is political science. Disregard my red hair and the bright clothes. I know I look more like a rock star than a would-be politician. But I plan on dying my hair black, changing my look, and becoming a powerful voice among the house or the senate."

"That is awesome. With hard work and dedication, I have no doubts about your success," Rohan replied, keeping a sharp focus on the young yet confident twenty year old. Monica gave a half smile then changed the subject. The young woman's interest in her husband seemed obvious. She hadn't taken her eyes off of him, and had yet to ask anything about his daughter. Or her for that matter.

Monica sometimes felt small and in the shadows. She was more than Rohan's wife. But it seemed everywhere they went all the fuss was made over Rohan. His presence forced her and her daughters into the shadows. A place she didn't mind dwelling in so long as the people within their immediate range did not forget that she existed.

"I'm Monica Jefferies. I'm a pediatrician. Well… retired pediatrician. I would like to wish you two the best at what this world has to offer. Study hard and push through the challenges and you will exit here victorious," she said. Sophie smiled then walked over to Avery and took her suitcase from her.

"Welcome…Let's get you situated. This is your bed and your side. The closet is small but we will work that out. My father is bringing me a huge storage unit designed just for college dorms. It's made of plastic and you can stack it and make it as big as you need."

"Your father?" Rohan questioned.

"Um…Yes sir. My father. He's all I have. I lost my mother pretty early on. I barely remember her. So it's just him and I."

"He drives from where?"

"He lives in Downtown Detroit."

"Oh! I see. Where does he work?" Rohan asked. Avery looked down. Once Rohan felt uncomfortable about something he had a thousand questions about it. It was apparent that he did not like the idea of Sophie's father making visits. Sophie was an adult and didn't need tons of visits. Shipping the unit or sending it by currier seemed the better choice.

Avery was appalled at the nerve of her father. If she could shrink or turn invisible, she would.

"He works for Ford," Sophie replied.

"As an engineer?" Rohan asked.

"No sir. He makes the cars."

"Oh. He works on the line," he asked, his eyes staring intensely. Monica could see that Sophie was starting to get uncomfortable.

"That's good honest work. Entire families survived off the *Big 3*. Right honey," Monica interjected.

She knew her husband well. He was as bougie as a man could get. It was an irritant at times, but Monica understood his need to keep certain people at bay. For him, it was a matter of *birds of a feather*. It was a simple mathematic equation. Successful people bred more success.

Monica watched as her daughter got more comfortable. It was good enough and she relaxed. They could exit and have a comfortable and worry-free drive back. Avery was happy and that was all that mattered. But Rohan was another issue. He seemed uncomfortable with the roommate and things in general. But this was him. Overbearing and sometimes, unreasonable.

"Well honey…we're going to go and let you get comfortable. If you need us you call. You have your credit cards. You have your things. If you need me to send something, just tell me and I will box it up and ship it. Alright?" Monica said, as she approached her daughter and hugged her.

"Yes mom. I will. I love you."

"I love you too."

"Love you baby," Rohan said, as he embraced Avery. She closed her eyes and for a second, questioned whether or not she was ready to make such a big move. Part of her wanted to take classes online and stay at home. But the last year had pushed her stress levels. Then the last two months made an even bigger impact and she settled on her original plan to break from the breasts of her mother, and grow up. She was now a woman and she wanted to make women type decisions.

"Bye," Avery waved as her parents pulled off. She stood in the parking lot with Sophie at her side, waving until they bent the corner and drove out of sight.

"Girl that was some weird shit. I like you and all, but your parents…Sheesh," she said. Avery gave her a look then after a few scary second, broke into laughter with Sophie relieved that she got the joke.

"I know right," Avery replied, as the two headed back to the dorm room and prepared for a first night away from home.

Chapter Two

The Perfect Family

"Mom!" Calista shouted, as she carried two year old Victoria in her arms.

"Coming! Hi honey. Let me see my grandbaby," she gloated as she took little Victoria from her daughter. Calista was the third born daughter. She held a law degree that collected dust on a shelf somewhere she couldn't recall. Working as a lawyer would put a dent in her already complex life that was made easy by her generous father.

"Your front door was wide open," Calista alerted.

"I know. I was on my way out to the garden but you know me…I get turned around," Monica said, bouncing her grand-daughter with delight. She was happy to see her family. It seemed Calista was becoming increasingly distant despite not having a job or a man to keep her busy. There was no excuse, yet she readily found one. Either she was with a mystery man or she was over one of her sister's houses. Monica preferred not to ask. She didn't believe her daughter but had nothing to prove otherwise.

Calista was a twenty five year old unmarried mother of one who was currently unemployed. Monica was at her wits end with her entitled and spoiled daughter who held a bachelor's degree and even passed the bar yet couldn't seem to find a suitable job. To make matters worse, Rohan was funding all her endeavors and had added her bills to theirs.

Monica did not know how to pry her indulgent husbands hands off the wheel. He had a need to take the steering wheel of everyone ride through life. She wanted her daughter to face her demons and step into the role of mother and degreed professional. But Rohan would rather just take care of her bills and keep up appearances.

Smokey Moment

"How's the job hunting going? Did you sign up through *Linked In* yet? That will be a valuable asset to your job hunting success."

"I know mom. I haven't found anything yet. A lot of the higher paying jobs want experience, which is what I lack. They also want advanced degrees which I also lack. My only options at this point would be to work for one of the automotive companies which dad hates. I just need to wait. Something will open up," Calista said with a tone meant to alert her mother as to her intolerance of the discussion.

It was the same question followed by the same answer and she was growing tired of her mother's insistence of inserting herself into the equation. Calista was sure her mother only mentioned it because of her father's generosities. She had tried and had no doubts she would find something soon. Until then, she wanted her mother to give her room and the chance to do it on her own without pressure.

"But you have your license to practice law."

"I know. I will find something. It's not a race mom."

"Jobs don't fall out of the sky Calista. You have to go after what you want. Beg them to give you an entry level position."

"Mom no! I'm not going to beg. I am the daughter of Rohan Jefferies. I'm not just taking anything."

"Ok honey. I'm not trying to upset you. I just want you to find something so you can stand on your own."

Calista looked off. She couldn't stand coming around at times because the line of questioning never went away. She longed for the day when she would be able to visit and relax without such conversations.

"Where's Avery? Was this the big day?" Calista asked.

"Actually, we took her last Friday. She's adjusting well," Monica noted.

"Is she?" Calista replied.

"Yes! Unless you know something I don't."

"I guess. Is dad here?"

"No…He'll be here soon though. You hungry?"

"No. I ate earlier. Just wanted to stop bye and bid Avery a good trip and start to a new life. She's going to do well. Did she pick a study?" Calista asked.

"For now, it's Liberal Arts. That will give her time to find her voice."

"Oh good. Well…I better get going. Tell dad I said hello. I'm going over Janine's for a minute so the kids can play, then I'm going home. Got a date tonight."

"Date? Who's watching Victoria?"

"Maybe Janine. I don't know yet. If not, I'll take her over my friend's house."

"No honey. Just leave her with me. I'm not that busy. I can watch her."

"It's ok mom. Janine wants to see her. I'm sure she'll agree to keeping her for a few hours," Calista said, as the sound of footsteps approached.

"Keeping who for a few hours?" Rohan said, as he walked to the kitchen counter and sat a bag full of groceries down. Calista was hoping to be gone by the time he came home. The absence of his car in the driveway was the deciding factor of her pop-up visit. Now her overbearing father had entered before she could escape his scrutiny.

"We we're just talking about Victoria. Calista 's going out and she's hoping Janine will watch the baby," Monica said.

"Leave her. We never see our grandbaby."

"Um…Janine is waiting on us. The kids want to see their cousin. I can't disappoint them. Maybe another day."

"You say that all the time. Another day. Well this is another day. Leave her. Janine sees Vic all the time. It's our turn," he said.

Monica looked down. The demands of her husband could be hard to take. She spent a lifetime defending her daughters against his harsh and controlling ways. Calista was the most sensitive of her girls. If Rohan pushed too hard, she would be a mess for days to come and it wouldn't be the first time.

Monica remembered that day so vividly. A middle of the night rage that had awakened her from a deep sleep had her running into a shouting match that made no sense and ended as quickly as it started. Calista ran away that night and stayed gone for three weeks. After missing persons reports and searches conducted by the police, Calista finally returned home. When she did, she was pregnant and exhausted. Calista was never the same.

“Let it be Rohan. She’s going to play with her cousins. I’m sure Victoria would rather play with her cousins, then hang out with grandma and grandpa,” Monica said.

“Nonsense. Let me see my baby,” Rohan said, picking up little Victoria. Calista gave her mother a sharp look. Her eyes were telling. She didn’t want to be ordered around by a narcissistic father bent on controlling his now grown daughters.

“She’s not staying dad. Sorry! We have to go,” Calista said taking her daughter from her father’s arms and walking towards the door. Rohan looked at his wife. It saddened him that his daughter showed such animosity towards him. It seemed he carried the weight of losing power with a family of girls that adored him growing up. Girls that had grown into women who now kept their distance.

He had only ever wanted the best for them. Now he fought for every minute to see them. For every second to be in his grandkid's lives. Monica seemed to side with her girls so there was never a win. Rohan was hurting inside. He wanted his family to heal. He wanted them to be tight. Close. They were all each other had.

"This not right Monica," he whispered.

"I know. She's having a hard time right now. Let me see her out honey," she said, as she followed behind her daughter. Calista stopped at the door and turned to her mother. She looked over her shoulder then back to her mother. Their eyes met in an intensity that Monica wasn't sure about. Calista appeared angry, but over what, was anyone's guess. It didn't take much for her third born daughter to feel threatened or voice a strong opinion over things other people would find simple and minor.

"Mom…I can't with him. It's the reason I don't even come here that much anymore. He always has to push. Always needs to have his way. He is your husband not mine. The only person submitting to him should be you."

"Calista! Why would you say that? Your father is not some monster. He is not that bad. He just wants his family close. He has nothing else. No siblings here. No friends really. All he has is us."

"And whose fault is that. He doesn't want friends. He was always too scared someone would be attracted to one of his daughters."

"Calista!"

"No mom. Enough is enough. I'm tired of playing normal when we are not a normal family. He's obsessed. If he wants family then why doesn't he called uncle Ziggy or uncle Lonnie and invite them here. He has brothers who are poor and struggle, while he lives a wealthy and entitled life. Why has he never tried to embrace them. Why? Where are his male friends? He is a member of congress. He is a member of a church. Yet there is no one. Why have we never had a cookout and invited people over. He's weird," she said, before Monica slapped her across the face. The action happened before she could think about it. Monica was horrified at her reaction but Calista's words were too much.

"I'm sorry baby," she said. Calista stood in shock, holding her face.

It was not surprising. After the words left her lips she felt the smack before it landed. Monica would allow only so much with regard to her beloved Rohan and bad mouthing him to an extreme was never allowed. Calista was forcing her hand and was ready to take whatever punishment fit the crime. Her father had ruined her life and she wanted her mother to know it. His controlling of every aspect of her had derailed what should be a normal existence under normal circumstances.

Her youth was spent at camp. Her teenage years spent under house study. The rule of *no outside company* only agitated the situation and forced the girls to sneak around instead of live openly and happily within the walls of their perfect looking home.

Calista slowly dropped her hand. A single tear fell as she shook her head in disbelief. Monica couldn't take it back She wished she could. Calista was slipping further away. It was taking her longer to visit and with this latest drama, she was sure her daughter would stay away even longer.

Smokey Moment

"I didn't mean it baby. I just hate to hear you bad mouth your father. He came here with nothing and built a life that people envy. You had everything growing up and you still have his help. It is through him you are able to live in your condo. It was his money that purchased your car. I know he is tough. He loves the only way he knows how. We love you no matter what," Monica said.

"I know mom. I just...," Calista said, as she turned and exited.

Monica stood in the doorway fighting back the onslaught of tears that were ready to be released. Her emotions poured from her like a fountain. Calista was delicate. She was going through something. The date she had planned probably wouldn't happen now. Calista held onto pain and took out her frustrations on those she loved. Monica wished her daughter would talk to her. Open up and explain the deep rooted pain that had no real basis that she could see.

Rohan was religious. He was also a *girl dad* and was highly protective of them. She saw the signs early on that he would smother their girls and tried to intervene, but Rohan would not allow the freedoms that Monica believed her girls should have. In the end, there was a compromise that she regretted. And now her house was empty, with Avery being the last of their four offspring, away at college. The house would be empty now and the couple would have to find something else to occupy their time. Their adult daughters had enough and was enjoying a life of autonomy. Monica couldn't blame them.

"You ok," Rohan said, as he walked up behind his wife.

"Yes. She's angry. She's so bitter. Were we really that bad of parents?"

"I don't know. I wish I had all the answers. I just wanted my girls protected. If you saw what I saw growing up as a child in Kingston you would understand why I was so intolerant. Girls are not protected. I promised myself that when I became a father, I would do everything in my power to protect my girls. Maybe I over shot my hand. Maybe I went too far. They resent me now."

"No baby, they don't. They just need time to figure things out for themselves. You are the best dad. I see you. I know you wanted nothing but the best for them. I know you take money from our account and buy them things. You still support them. Give them a chance to figure it out on their own. Maybe you should pull back with some of the support. I sometimes feel like they resent us carrying on over them. Janine is twenty nine. Roxanne is twenty seven. Calista is twenty five. Now our baby is off to college. She'll be nineteen very soon. We've done our job. We can relax. Do us. Travel. Do more with the church."

"Are you saying don't pay their bills?"

"Yes. That's exactly what I'm saying. Let them go. They must spread their wings. This is for their own good. Maybe Calista will stop stalling and get a job. Janine too. You brought her a Range Rover for her birthday. That is excessive honey. I hate to say this to you but its time. Let them be self-sufficient. Calista will get it together when she is forced to. She is the most spoiled. She wants everything handed to her. Let he do it herself."

Chapter Three

Family Drama

Monica rubbed lotion between her fingers to soften the delicate skin of her overworked hands. She was once again thinking of hiring a maid. The Jeffries were wealthy. She wanted what came with such a fortune. The staff she once had all left one by one. Only the housekeeper remained. But then one day she was ordered out of the house and Monica found herself void of any staff.

There was no chef. There was no housekeeper. There wasn't a chauffeur. Only one on standby. Rohan drove himself except on special occasions when he wanted to make a grand entrance.

It was days like this she regretted listening to him. She wished she fought to keep her housekeeper Eveline, on board. Her experience and five years with the family was wonderful. Eveline was everything. A smart, witty and energetic woman from Australia who loved them like family. One day Rohan woke on the wrong side of the bed and ordered Eveline out of their home. He stated words that didn't make much sense but that was Rohan. He ran a tight ship. It was his money. It was his connections. So things would run his way.

"Hey hun. You ready to turn in," Monica asked her husband as she entered his office. She could smell the Cuban cigar from the hallway.

"Huh," he said, clicking away on his computer and then closing everything out for the evening.

"Just asking if you were ready to go to bed. There are some new movies we can watch. Maybe something kinky. I put on your favorite perfume," she said, sitting on his desk and opening her legs to give him a better view.

"Mhmmm. You did. Come here. Sit on my lap. I want to smell you," he said. Monica sat in his lap and scoot close to his groin. She was limber and still very agile for a forty five year old. Her perfectly styled short hair that laid neatly on the sides and spiked just slightly in the top looked gorgeous on her.

Monica was all natural. Her thin athletic frame was kept up by a persistent need to eat right and exercise in their home gym. Many of her church sister's, longtime friends and family members attributed her commitment to working out to her desire to keep Rohan's eyes from roaming. Although he'd never been caught in an uncompromising position, many believed he was just being careful.

There were whispers of him being a man with so much to choose from, that he had to be guilty of at least one affair. Monica never listened to idle gossip. She knew that although her man was over fifty, he was also still very much attractive and fit. He was gorgeous and she knew it. Whispers were just signs of jealousy and Monica was aware of a woman's desire to see another woman's marriage fail. That, plus money to spare, made him a target. Monica was in fact, working to keep the fires burning.

Things between them had slowed despite them being in a better position to indulge each other. A house with four young girls constantly running around, made it hard to light fires that would turn into roaring flames. But now there was no excuse. She would indulge him and make those fires burn bright. She could see his smoldering eyes scan her body. She wanted him. He wanted her. Her warm uncovered vagina caused him to get an erection, and she would get what she wanted.

Rohan pulled her closer and pulled his large and erect manhood from his pants. Monica stood then slowly mounted him, moaning, as she eagerly anticipated each inch that entered her. Rohan held her face and looked her over as if studying her.

"You are so beautiful. How can a man be so lucky," he said, staring into her eyes with intense purpose.

Monica smiled then stood on her tip toes as she moved forward against his body. She rocked back and forth, throwing her head back, as she enjoyed the smells and sounds of her sexually charged life partner. He was everything. Monica couldn't think of a time she didn't want him. No matter what, sex was never off the tables.

She was addicted to his size. His girth. The tip. The shaft. Every single inch of his ten inch cock did it for her. It had been a while since they'd had sex somewhere other than the bed. But Monica feared losing her grip. This was just the beginning. Now that Avery was gone, she would be opening her legs in the shower. In the kitchen. In the grand room. And anywhere else when the mood hit. This was the start of a second phase in their life.

"Mhmmm daddy," Calista moaned, as she opened her legs wider for the pummeling that her new beau KC was giving. He pounded her insides like raw meat and she felt she was in love. It had been a while since someone had done her pussy right although it had not been that long since she'd had sex. Vince was no good at sex and only ate a mean pussy. Rashad had a big dick, but was clueless as to how to use it. Then there was Michael. The son of a millionaire financier. Everything was fine until he went to kiss her, and she nearly fell-out from the smell that radiated from his mouth. He called her dozens of times afterward until he finally gave up.

"Whose pussy is this?" KC asked. Calista rolled her eyes and then snickered causing him to stop abruptly.

"Something funny?" he asked.

"What? No.... It's nothing. Keep going," she replied.

"Keep going?" KC said.

"Yes! What! Gotdamn…Just…," Calista said pushing him off of her and grabbing her robe.

"Every time we fuck you say or do some foul shit. You laughed at me while I'm trying to please you. Like really laughed at a nigga. What the fuck be up with you?" he said.

"Nothing KC. Your sensitive. Can't laugh. Can't smile. Can't talk nasty. You analyze everything. It's all good. We're having fun. What's the big deal?"

"Fun? We're having fun?"

"Yes, fun. I don't see you complaining."

"I'm complaining now Calista. You don't take me seriously. I'm not a piece of fucking meat. You call me for fuck sessions and won't even let me spend the night. You kick me out right after. Now you laugh. This some game you play with niggas. No wonder you single."

"Fuck you!"

"Naw bitch, fuck you! I'm sick of the games. You think because you pretty with a body that a nigga gone let you do and say whatever. I aint cut like that," KC said, as he stood and started getting dressed.

"Ya'll all just alike. You aint no fucking unicorn," Calista said, looking down. KC stopped and stared. He was angry beyond his normal limits.

"I'm leaving before I do something I'll regret. Don't you ever fucking call me. You don't know me if you see me on the streets. Crazy bitch! You got that…You don't know me! I regret the day I fucking met yo ass. Thought I found something special. I aint find shit! Another foul-mouthed hoe opening her legs with no meaning behind it. It's bitches like you that make it bad for the real ones," he said, as he zipped his vintage True Religions.

He pulled his tee shirt over his head and then grabbed his Rolex. Calista felt bad. She didn't really want him to leave. She couldn't tell him that she was her own worst nightmare. That she said those things to keep from loving him. It was all an act. All things she had done before. Before the love. Before he would have the chance to break her heart. And before her overbearing father came around and ruined it.

KC walked down the hall towards the front door. He could hear footsteps behind him.

"KC wait! Please…I'm sorry," Calista said. He kept his back to her then sighed and continued on.

"Wait! Wait," she said, running behind him. KC turned around and stared intensely at her. He was beginning to believed she was slightly touched.

"Wait for what? What is it Calista? You not done making me feel bad. Something else about my lovemaking makes you laugh?"

"No."

"Then what…I got shit to do."

"I'm scared of this."

"What!"

"I laugh when I'm nervous. Something about you scares me. I don't know how to move forward. I don't know what you want."

"I want you! What the fuck Calista. There's no hide and seek going on. I'm not keeping anything from you. I give you my all and you keep me hidden. I can't do this with you. You need help. I can tell you have pain. Probably some nigga broke your heart. You have to get that shit in order. Find what it is you want. It aint me," he said. Calista walked slowly towards him.

"But it is you," she said, walking within an inch from him. She looked at his mouth then back to his piercing eyes. KC was a dream. His brown smooth skin, perfectly trimmed goatee and beard and his neat, short cornrows gave off a rough and sexy vibe. He was six feet tall, towering over her like a skyscraper. His physique was perfect. All muscle, bulked up just right. He looked good. He smelled good. And he did it, in ways no other ever did. Calista was not willing to lose him. He was right. She needed to get herself together. Pain covered her like wrapping paper. She was surprised he saw it. It meant he was empathic. That he could feel her. He couldn't leave. She had unknowingly fallen in love.

"I know what I want," she said, kissing him slowly then moving down his body until she was on her knees. Calista snatched his pants and forced his zipper down. She pulled his dick from his pants and gave it a teasing lick. "I want this. And you. And everything good that we find together," she said, looking up at him. She kept her gaze on him as she swallowed him whole.

KC dropped his head and closed his eyes. Calista had kept this treat from him. Despite him eating her pussy more than once, she had yet to give him her mouth. It was now his favorite place. Calista had him sweating within a few short strokes. KC knew he couldn't leave. He wasn't sure how bad it would get, before he would leave a woman with a mouth made of gold.

"Don't leave me," Calista said.

"Girl, I aint going no fucking were. Now… Don't stop. Gotdamn…Do that thing again," he said. Calista tucked him back in neatly then pulled him out and spit on the tip. What came next felt like sexual battery in the best way. Her manipulation of his shaft and head using her tongue, jaws and hands took him from ten to one hundred quickly.

"Fuckkkk girl. You gonna make a nigga cum. What the fuck you doing to me. Who you been sucking like that?" he said, as he held her head and pushed himself to the back of her throat.

"Gotdamnnn. Where you get that from," he said, looking down at her. Calista was in another world. KC had done it all. He had women from the east coast to Miami and out west near places like Los Angeles and the Bay. In all his travels, one-night stands and private parties where anything went, no one had given head like Calista. Her abilities went towards porn star status. KC was fascinated. He was hooked. Calista was now the mystery box he planned to unwrap. There was something about her. An element hidden that made her unique. He was ready to peal her like an onion. He was now a dope fein and Calista was his fix.

Chapter Four

An Uneasy Feeling

"Right here bae," Calista instructed KC, as they pulled up to Janine's condo. The two had become inseparable and Janine, Roxanne and their mother Monica had been calling her. They were filled with worry, wondering why she was missing in action. Calista was leaving Victoria with Janine for days at a time and now the family was curious. Janine didn't mind.

She had practically raised Victoria the first six months while Calista tried adjusting to motherhood. Now Janine had a worry of a different sort. Calista was leaving Victoria for longer than she should and Janine wanted to look her in the eyes. Calista had a history of self-medicating and Janine hoped she hadn't relapsed.

"Well hello," Janine greeted. Calista and KC were all smiles. Janine instantly felt a sense of relief. Calista didn't look high or under the influence of anything.

"Are you going to let us in," Calista asked, as she looked her sister over and snickered then wrapped her arm in KC's and gave her sister a look.

"Hmph. So is this why I can't get a call. A visit. Nothing. He's the reason Victoria can't come home," Janine said, looking curiously at the handsome man her sister seemed thrilled about.

"Janine this is KC. KC this is my sister Janine."

"Nice to meet you," KC said.

"Likewise," Janine replied, looking him over once more. It didn't take a brilliant mind to see KC was for the streets. His tattoos, tattered expensive looking jeans, white tee, jewelry and Jordan's left little to guess about. He looked dipped in trouble and sprinkled with extra naughty. Janine imagined he was tearing her sister a new asshole from the looks of the bulging print seated nicely at his groin.

"Are you going to let us in or do you plan on standing there," Calista said.

"Oh sorry. My manners," Janine said, as she moved to the side.

◆

"Nice place," KC said to Janine, as he waited on Calista to return from the bathroom. Janine gave a half smile. She didn't like street guys. She didn't like that their lives usually spilled into the lives of others. It was hard keeping a pleasant face when she really wanted to cut things short and see him to the door. But Janine had no dig in the fight. Victoria was welcomed to stay for as long as needed. She also liked that Calista appeared happy. It had been a minute since she'd seen that smile.

"Thanks. I was sold on the square footage. I am a sucker for size. I mean…You know what I mean," she said, looking off as the embarrassment of the words made her feel awkward. KC smiled then took a sip of his cognac. Soon a knock interrupted them. Janine stood up.

"Excuse me," she said. KC watched her walk towards her door. Janine was built like something out of a magazine. Her ample ass was much rounder than Calista's but he wouldn't trade. Not with Calista scoring so high on the scale of bedroom skills. Still she was beautiful. Something in her cool and relaxed demeanor was sexy. Unlike Calista who was quirky, blunt and aggressive in nature.

"Sorry we're late honey. Your dad wanted to stop and get a bottle of the best. You know he loves his cognac," Monica said. KC stood up. It was apparent that the woman was Calista's mother.

"Ma, this is KC," Janine said.

"Oh…A friend of yours?" she asked.

"No. He came with Calista."

"Hello young man. I'm Calista's mom. Her father is…Well he was right behind me," she said. Suddenly the door closed. The sound of firm and purposeful footsteps came down the hall. The distinguished and handsome Rohan, with his signature salt and pepper hair, emerged. KC was impressed. The man was dressed elegantly and looked good for a man his age. KC put him somewhere in his late fifties even though he was ageing well.

"Honey come meet Calista's boyfriend," Monica said. Rohan furrowed. KC stared keenly. The man didn't seem too happy to meet. His long pause was still going on even as he walked towards the group. Suddenly Calista emerged from the back of the condo.

"He's not my boyfriend. We're just friends. There isn't a commitment or anything. Jeez Janine," she said.

"That's not what it looked like to me," Janine replied. KC looked at Calista, locking eyes with her for a brief time. Her quick move to shoot down any connection between them had not gone unnoticed.

"I'm Congressman Rohan Jeffries. And you are?" he asked.

"KC, sir."

"Does that stand for something?" Rohan asked, as he shook KC's hand slowly.

"No. People call me KC. Since I was a kid. Never been called anything else," he said.

"KC. Alright then," Rohan said, pulling his hand away. He turned his attention to Calista and gave a visual reprimand. He wasn't pleased. He stepped away from the crowd and carried the small bag with a special box of liquor inside and headed for his daughter's kitchen.

"I'll help him," Monica said, as Janine and Calista looked at each other. KC wasn't sure why the mood changed. There was something in the air now that the parents had arrived. Part of him shrugged it off to parents who were still forcing their opinions on their adult children. He wouldn't know. His father was in jail and his mother was a drug abuser who he kept his distance from.

"Um…So we could um…Go out on my terrace. It's beautiful. I have a great view of the pond," Janine said.

"That's a good idea," Calista replied, picking up her and KC's drinks and following her sister outside. KC was still feeling slighted by the abrupt manners of Rohan. Calista could see that her father had managed to change the mood of the party. She spoke up quickly before KC sunk any lower into the abyss.

"Sorry babe. My father is a complete asshole. He just doesn't know how to make people feel accepted," Calista said, as she looked at the glass door to ensure her father was not close by.

"I get it bae. He's just protective. All fathers should be protective of their daughters. As I spend time with Victoria, I'm going to feel protective of her. It's my job," he said. Calista took a sip of her cognac and smiled nervously. Janine looked at her then at KC.

"So… marriage is in the cards for you two?" Janine asked.

"I think so," KC replied.

"I was just asking because men should not play father unless they are the father," Janine said. KC was taken aback once again. He looked at Calista.

"I didn't mean anything by that. I was just saying men should protect girls," KC replied.

"Yeah…They should," Janine said, picking the olive from her Martini and popping it in her mouth. She stood up and excused herself then went back inside her condo. KC looked off. He could see where Calista got her abrupt and cold tone from. Her family was brutal. It seemed they did not like outsiders.

"Is it me or does your entire family hate me?" he whispered, looking through the glass watching out for anyone headed their way. Calista's eyes jumped around. She was speechless, which was puzzling, given that Calista was never without a response.

"Did I do something?"

"No! No bae…I should have warned you about him. He is a powerful man. He dines with judges and senators. He wants to run for president one day. Thinks he'll be the next Barack Obama," she said, laughing nervously, as she trembled slightly. KC couldn't make heads or tails of what he was seeing. But powerful or not, this was her father. She should be used to his ways. It was hard to make sense of a twenty five year old woman acting like her daddy would spank her. He still hadn't gotten past her denial of their relationship. If she was going to deny them, why bring him. KC thought about things. it was another red flag. His mind raced. He realized something but wanted to be clear.

"He wasn't supposed to be here was he?"

"What?"

"I'm asking if you knew he was coming here today?" KC reiterated.

"Um…No, he wasn't. But it doesn't matter."

"But see Cali, it does."

"How?"

"It means you weren't prepared to introduce us and I want to know why. You act like you're a minor and I'm breaking some law. You're not seventeen. You're twenty five. I'm twenty nine. Like… two grown ass muthafuckas."

"Keep your voice down," Calista said, looking behind her.

"I just want to know why the secrecy. Why was I only supposed to meet your sister?"

"Because Janine is…She's just Janine. She has a good heart. She sees things clearly. She supports me. I wasn't ready for you to meet anyone else."

"That goes for your daughter as well. Right?" he asked.

"Don't bring Victoria up. That's…That's not up for discussion. Victoria is only two. You will meet her one day. Just not now," Calista said, her eyes searching his for understanding. KC leaned back. He looked out at the horizon. Calista was too much for him to process. The closer he felt they were becoming, the more he realized how distant they truly were.

"I should go. I have to do something. I'll call you later," KC said. Calista had no words. She really didn't want him exposed to her overbearing father for a second longer. She was sure he wasn't done grilling him and she wanted to spare him the stings.

"Alright."

"Can you get home from here?" he asked.

"Of course. I think Roxanne coming. If not, Janine will take me back home. Will I see you tonight?"

"Are you sure you want to?" he asked.

Calista paused. He sounded serious and she was not ready for any back and forth with him, especially with Rohan lurking.

"Yes, I do. Of course," she said.

KC threw back the last in his tumbler then walked back inside. Calista was heartbroken. She felt she was losing her power over him. Her family was hard to handle. It was why she had no interest in bringing him around too early. But dating in private was hard with a family that wanted to know everything. Calista's eyes swelled with tears. She hurried and wiped them hoping she didn't get caught. She would never hear the end of it.

"It's nice out here," Rohan said, as he slid the glass door to the side and slid it back closed.

"Yes it is. Where is everybody?" Calista asked.

"Well…Janine has company. Two of her girlfriends just showed up. Your mom is talking them to death. You know how she is. She lives for these moments," he said. Calista smiled as she kept her eyes gazing out in the distance.

She could feel something coming. Her father wasn't subtle with what he thought or how he felt about something.

"That young man seems nice," he said.

"He is."

"Where does he work?" he asked.

"He's self employed dad. He owns properties."

"How did he get the money to acquire the property? A job, right? Where did he used to work?" he asked.

"Dad! Come on. I just met him. I didn't interview him. These are things you find out over time. Right now he owns property. Anything else I need to know will come with time," she said, her voice taking on a hint of weightiness.

"That's where you are wrong. You are the daughter of a congressman. Possibly the president. I raised you to get to the bottom of anyone who holds importance in your life. You have currency… Your face. Your womanly ways. And your name. It is all currency that anyone would want to cash in on. You can't entertain the likes of men like him without…," he said before being cut off.

"Men like him! You don't know him!"

"I don't need to know him. I can see. He is a hoodlum. There, I said it. A hoodlum who has no place in your life."

"No one does. You want me alone. Nothing…Nobody!"

"That's not true."

"Oh no," Calista said, her eyes piercing his with a cold stare he hadn't seen. Monica could see the look from the living room and started towards them. Janine followed her. They could see the two were in a heated conversation.

"I don't have to listen to this," Calista said.

"Don't you turn your back on me. This is your rebellion talking. You could care less about that boy. You'll do anything to go against me," he said. Monica slid the door open and stepped out.

"Rohan please! I thought we weren't going to say anything about it," she said.

"What! So you two were talking about me?" Calista said.

"No no honey. We were just saying that this KC guy is not quite on your level. That's all. Nothing serious. If you like him then by all means, have fun. Just be careful."

"Careful?"

"Yes honey. Your father and I only want the best for you."

"Really?"

"Yes. Why would you think anything else. It's not a bad thing to want the best for you and your sisters," Monica said. Calista looked at Janine and laughed.

"You hear that. They want what's best for us," Calista said. Janine shook her head side to side. Whatever road Calista was going down, she wanted no parts of it.

"Calista calm down. It's really not a big deal," Janine said. Just then a knock at the door pulled Janine from the middle of the drama. Calista picked up her drink and emptied it then slammed the tumbler on the patio table.

"I'm going to call myself an Uber. Enjoy the rest of your evening," Calista said, walking past her parents. She slid the glass door then got emotional when she saw their sister Roxanne.

"Roxie," she said, bolting to her and hugging her tight.

Roxanne was beautiful, with silky hair and beautiful eyes that gave off an Asian-Black mix. Her curvy figure amped up her appeal even as she tried to tone it down. Her small waist and thick butt and thighs were hard to cover though she did a good job. Suits and dresses that were more on the modest side, were her staple. Her enviable figure was the result of Monica and Rohan's good genes. All the Jeffries girls had shapes. They were also blessed with a silky grade of hair. Roxanne's legs were flawless and she enjoyed the powerful femme fatale look of a skirt-suit with heels.

"You alright?" Roxanne whispered in Calista's ear as she held their embrace.

"Yeah. He's at it again. Trying to control everything. I can't take him. I hate him," she whispered.

Roxanne looked at her father with coarse eyes. Her stare was deadly. Of all the Jeffries children, Roxanne was the one to fear. She was highly intelligent, gifted and skilled in the art of war. A verbal argument with her felt more like a verbal assault. An altercation would not go well for the intended target and so it was best to steer clear of her.

Roxanne was too busy climbing the corporate ladder to indulge Rohan or her mother in their attempts to continue raising grown children. Instead of accepting a person's choices, they pushed for change. Roxanne had tired of it and kept her visits down to just a few a year. Holidays and birthdays to be exact. Anything more would be too much. Therapy had helped her come to grips with her childhood. Now distance helped her maintain her sanity.

"You remember what I told you?" Roxanne asked, as she pulled away and leaned back.

"Yes," Calista replied.

"Use that. Each and every time," she said. Janine furrowed. She wasn't sure what Roxanne meant and made a mental note to ask her later.

"Dad," Roxanne greeted.

"How's my girl. They treating you right over at Penntoil?" he asked. Roxanne was an executive for an oil company. Between stocks, bonds, real estate and earning, she was bringing in over a million dollars a year. Rohan was proud of her. He bragged endlessly about her accomplishments. Janine was doing well too. But no one was doing as well as Roxanne.

"Yes. We continue to see record numbers each quarter. This will be our best year yet. Hi mom?" Roxanne said, changing to a warm smile.

Roxanne loved her mother immensely. Nothing in their past would erase it. She understood that her father was a controlling narcissist who kept a tight leash on his wife and children. Those days were long gone for her. She just wished her sisters would remove themselves from his power.

"Hi baby. I was just about to pull everything out of the oven. You ready to relax with a drink and some delicious food?" Monica asked her second born.

"Oh yes. Definitely! Do you need help?"

"I can do it mom. Did everyone forget this is my house?" Janine said.

Roxanne chuckled and walked with Calista towards the terrace. Rohan stood for a minute. He wasn't sure where to go. Whether he should follow his girls out onto the terrace, or follow Janine and his wife into the kitchen. In the end he decided to sit on the couch with Janine's friends Suki and Cleo.

"You sure you ok?" Roxanne asked. She was protective of Calista. She lived in fear of her younger sister relapsing under the weight of life and the things not under her control. She had tried to get Calista to go to therapy with her, but was unable to convince her. Calista was a wild flower. She did her own thing. But she was also an empath who felt things deeply. Roxanne promised herself she would never give up trying to get Calista to talk to professionals instead of keeping things bottled up inside.

"Yes. He ran my date off. KC picked up on his bullshit and just couldn't get comfortable after that," Calista said.

"You have to keep your life away from dad. He will never approve. Not even if you married the president. He says he will. He will not! Just remember to meditate. Pray. And keep away. My therapist said there is nothing wrong with divorcing your parents if things get too toxic. Either you take him on and shut him down, or you get the fuck away from him. Do like I did. He don't fuck with me! I got a whole girlfriend at home and he will not weigh in on it. All that mumbo jumbo about lesbians being the servants of Satan. Remember he used to say that. He has not said that shit to me not one time. He knows I would go ham on that ass," Roxanne said.

Calista burst into laughter. She loved Roxanne's strong presence. She was feminine all the way, but she was strong when it came to her personal space, her mental health and her privacy. Roxanne was in a five year relationship with a woman she met in college. The woman was as close to a man as Roxanne wanted to get. She'd never been with a man sexually and Calista wondered why her sister never even tried.

They spoke about marrying a man when they grew up. Talks of finding someone like their father. But Roxanne ended up switching gears. It was fine. Calista could care less. She didn't have the nerve to ask the question. Roxanne didn't like to talk about anything she deemed private and no one's business, which was just about every subject. Being her sister did not mean a free and open invitation to prying into her affairs. Calista figured on day Roxanne would talk. One day she would say what changed in her that led to her being engaged to a woman.

"How's Hazel?" Calista asked.

"Good. She had to go to Arizona on business. I miss my baby. She's supposed to come back Saturday," Roxanne said.

Calista nodded and turned her attention to a family of geese in the lake. Roxanne felt her phone buzz and checked it. The gesture made Calista realize she hadn't checked her phone.

"Where is my phone?" Calista said, standing and looking around. She walked around the porch, checking under the table then walked back inside the condo. She hoped it was somewhere obvious. If it was lost it wouldn't be the first time.

"Oh here it is," she said, as she picked it up and checked her messages. She saw a text from KC. The time was marked twenty minutes prior, which meant he sent it as soon as he left. The message read:

Listen. I can feel something is off. I don't like family drama. If a woman's family don't like me, I can't be around them. I'm not going to fake like I'm cool with someone. Your people do not like me. Your father looked at me like I was a roach he needed to squish. So before I get myself into some trouble, I'm going to pull out. I can't be responsible for what I will say or do if he gets disrespectful one day. Sorry Cali. I really thought you were the one.

Calista dropped her hand, as she held onto the phone. Tears formed in her eyes as she tried to balance out her uncontrolled emotions. Soon her eyes met her fathers. He narrowed his gaze as Calista shook her head at him then turned and walked back to the terrace. She looked back once. The look on his face almost appeared like a faint smirk. It was irritating to see. He had purposeful set out to make KC uncomfortable and it worked. His mission was accomplished. Her relationship ended just as fast as it had started and she could strangle her father.

"Can you run me home. I have to go," she said.

"Of course. Is something wrong?" Roxanne asked.

"I'll tell you in the car. Right now I just want to leave."

◆

Monica walked to the back of her daughter's huge condo. She wanted to see the updates that Janine did. Her luxurious home was spectacular. Monica smiled as she entered her granddaughters, Shelby and Taylor's room. Their pink and yellow decorated space was bright and fun. She walked over to the dresser.

Papers sat in a neat pile. Monica figured Janine was getting organized. She walked to the dresser and picked up a picture her grandkids and Rohan. It was a picture she didn't know existed. It looked as though he had taken them somewhere fun. Monica furrowed. She was jealous and she had all sorts of thoughts on it. She would have wanted to go.

Janine barely brought her kids around and Monica tired of seeing them only on holidays. She wanted to be their babysitter but Janine said she had them in early education programs. Now it seemed Rohan had a special day with the girls and she wondered why he would take them somewhere and make sure to include her. Not even tell her. Her mind began to race. Soon thoughts of logical explanations made her feel somewhat at ease.

"Hey I was looking for you," Janine said, as she entered.

"Oh honey sorry. Just admiring your place. The girls room is so nice," Monica said. Janine stared at the picture she held.

"Oh, I saw this sitting here. When did Rohan take the kids out?" she asked.

"Oh um…He didn't take them. I had taken them to a festival and dad called to check on them. When I told him where I was he said he was close by and he actually just came for a minute."

"Oh," Monica said, looking back at the picture. Rohan held the youngest as Janine held Taylor. It was a strange pose. Monica was uncomfortable for the first time but she wasn't sure why. Why the image of him with Janine and her girls bothered her. Something in their pose. Something in his face as he looked at Janine. It was a look that men gave to the women they loved. Eyes that spoke of something more.

Smokey Moment

"Lets' go finish the food. Everybody's hungry," Janine said.

Monica followed her out, struggling to stop strange thoughts from entering. This was their daughter. Of course, he loved her. He loved his family with ever fiber in his being. It couldn't be anything. Rohan's face was expressive. He wore his feeling on the outside. Whatever he was feeling that day would show through. His powerful eyes gave themselves away. If he liked you, it showed. If he hated you, it showed. There was no guessing with him. And it was obvious he adored Janine.

Monica shook it off. Janine was always his favorite. Her daughter was private and didn't give much by way of her personal. Monica envisioned a daughter who had gotten closer to her father and was perhaps sharing more with him than her. Maybe Rohan felt a special bond because of that. They didn't even know who the kid's father was. Janine never said. Monica relaxed. If they had somehow grown closer then that was a good thing. Janine needed someone to confide in. She didn't want her eldest child to keep all that there was about her life bottled up.

“Alright, let’s get this stuff on the table,” Monica said, as she entered the kitchen.

“Yes. Let’s eat,” Janine replied, as she grabbed a tray. The women started carrying the food into the dining room.

“Alright let’s eat. It looks fabulous Janine,” Rohan said with a smile.

“Thanks dad.”

Chapter Five

Unbreakable Bonds

Monica rode the elevator to the 9th floor. She looked like royalty in her pink blouse, white slacks and black and white shoes. She carried a pink clutch and wore a wide flashy pink tourmaline and gold necklace. Whispers of her being the mother of the company's number one executive filled the air. Monica felt proud. She could see everyone's attention on her and she knew why. Her daughter had single handedly turned their company around through clever marketing and opening channels with smaller companies who had already closed their doors.

"I'm here to see my daughter, Roxanne Jeffries," she said.

"Sure! Take a seat and I will let her know you are here," the woman said. Monica walked over to a lounge area and sat down. She crossed her legs and got comfortable. Roxanne had done a lot in a short amount of time and it showed.

"Mom! Hi…What are you doing here? You trying to take me to lunch?" Roxanne asked.

"Yes. Do you have time?" she asked.

"I'll make time. Let me go talk to my boss. I'll be ready in a second," Roxanne said.

Monica waited, walking slowly through the lounge area admiring the oil paintings on the wall. Soon Roxanne emerged from the back with her Louis Vuitton leather crossbody and her cell phone.

The women walked to the corner and crossed the street. A delicious café sat near the corner of Main and Nineth

Street. Roxanne walked in to the greetings and smiles of the staff who were already familiar with her.

"Table for two?" the waitress asked.

"Yes. Thank you."

Roxanne and Monica took a seat and got comfortable. Monica folder her hands realizing that her daughter would have to get back to work at some point. She didn't want to be so bold and dump but she also had no time. She wanted more time than she assumed she had. Plus, Roxanne was her most challenging daughter as far as information. She could take a secret to her grave. Monica hoped Roxanne would be honest.

"I'm sorry to pop up on you sweetheart. Somethings been bothering me," she said. Roxanne leaned in and took her mother's hand.

"What? Why you look so serious? Is it dad?" she asked.

"Yes. I want to know what happened that day at Janine's condo. You looked at your father like you could kill him. Calista was upset. Janine was acting weird. I know your father wasn't easy to live with. He's has his ways, but he means well. What bothers me is you girls are grown. I still call you my girls but that is an endearing term. You all are women. But just because you're grown doesn't mean I take my eyes off of you. I notice things. You all are harboring a dislike for your father and I want to know what I can do to facilitate a truce. I want to have a family meeting," she said.

Roxanne stared at her mother then slowly pulled her hands back. As she prepared to speak, the waitress returned with water and menus.

"You know what you want or will you need a minute?" the waitress asked.

"Please give us a minute?" Roxanne replied. The waitress walked away and Roxanne took her time to think about a response.

"Everybody got pain. That's life. Yes, he was hard to live with. Controlling. Overbearing. Strict to the point of excessive. He made my life hell. And I can tell you from the conversations I've had with Calista he practically destroyed her. Janine is more neutral. She seems to have found her peace. Avery is too young to express herself in a way that makes sense. She copes by playing video games and talking to her friends. A family meeting won't solve anything mom. It is past stuff and you can't recall the past or change it. Only thing you can do is get closure or get therapy. I got my therapy a long time ago. And I don't want to talk to a man who has not changed. That kind of parenting is abusive mom. It's abuse. So when you ask me why I looked at him in that way, now you know. He abused us. And I find it hard to show him compassion. I'm still working through the pain. But I have flashbacks every now and then and I can't help that."

"Is that why you shut us out of your life?"

"No ma! I didn't shut anyone out. I'm just living my life the best way I know how. I'm just being Roxanne. Please understand that," she said.

"Oh baby, I do. I just wished we could get a redo. Maybe if I had been more demanding with him, you guys wouldn't feel this way."

Roxanne took a swallow of water and held her mother's hand once more.

"How could you have helped us when he abused you too?" she asked. Monica's eyes widened from shock. She had no immediate reaction to her daughter's strong words.

"Oh Roxie," Monica said, as tears fell from her eyes.

"You have to admit it first, then you will be able to see our pain. The fact that you are asking me this lets me know you have not processed it correctly. You have blinders on mom. He was a horrible husband. He still is. You act like you don't see him. Do you even know him? Really see him?"

"Yes…I..I... Of course I do. That's my husband of twenty six years. Rohan is not as terrible as you girls think. He just wanted the best for you. Is that so bad?" she asked.

"Why is Avery away at school?" Roxanne asked.

"What?"

"I'm asking why did she go away to school. She was adamant about going to college locally and staying home. Now she is in a dorm in Michigan, away from family. Like there are no colleges here in Ohio. When was that decided?"

"By her. What are you saying?"

"I'm saying that it's not the conversation we had. This was not her plan. Now things have changed and she made a major move."

"She changed her mind. She came to me and asked that I help her get in a dorm at U of M."

"That's all?" Roxanne asked.

"Yes. What else would there be?"

'Nothing. I better order. I have to get back mom. I do have a meeting scheduled."

"Oh yes baby. Sorry," she replied.

"Don't be sorry. I'm glad we had this talk. I just hope you slow down and pay closer attention. Especially to Calista and Avery. They're not as strong as Janine and I. Calista is in crisis and Avery has something going on."

"Something going on? Is there something you're not telling me?"

"No! She won't talk to me and I don't have time to drive all the way to Ann Arbor Michigan. I figure she'll talk when she's ready. All I know is everyone eventually gets away from him," Roxanne said

"That was not nice Roxie."

"It's true mom. And I don't see how you could let him touch you."

"That is my husband!"

"I know. But the ring shouldn't be a blinder."

"I'm not blind to anything Roxanne. I know he is difficult."

"It's ok mom. He is your husband at the end of the day. I don't want you to get upset. I just want you to be aware. There is a reason for our anger."

"I just don't see it that way," Monica said.

"I know."

Calista drove down McMicken Ave headed to where she hoped KC was. His barber shop was just a few more miles down. He didn't actually cut hair, but did go there and spend time. He wasn't answering her calls and this visit was necessary. She hoped he didn't unleash his anger on her for ignoring his wishes. His follow up text solidified the first one and he doubled down on his original words that stated he was done.

"His car is here," she mumbled to herself, as she parked next to it. A tall figure walked past the windows. It was KC. Calista kept her eyes on him. Soon he broke into laughter as a woman approached and hit him on the arm. KC grabbed his arm in a dramatic fashion and pretended to be injured. Calista flew into a rage.

KC could see her serious and purposeful march as she neared his door. He tried to beat her to it so he could exit, but Calista was fast.

"I called you," she said, looking past him at the woman who hit him on the arm. The woman erupted into a light and playful laughter and Calista blew up.

"Keep your hands off of him."

"Oh hell naw KC. Who is this bitch standing in my salon telling me what I can and can't do with my baby daddy. That's right. We have a son. I'll hit him. Kick him. Punch his ass if I want. You aint gone do shit. That's for damn sure."

"Enough Keisha!" KC shouted. "Let's go outside," he said, pulling Calista by the arm.

"Go on now. You better just go. Cause if you keep giving me that look, I'm going to remove yo gotdamn eyeballs," Keisha said.

"Do it bitch! I want to see that shit. Come on. Show me," Calista said.

"Cali stop. Keisha…Stop that shit. I'm not playing," he said. KC pulled Calista outside then grabbed her by the arm and walked to the end of the building.

"What the fuck Cali. For real though? You didn't get my text," he asked.

"Yeah."

"And…,"

"And what. You just leave me because I got a mean ass daddy. He doesn't have anything to do with us."

"It's more than that dammit! It's you Cali. You!" KC said, stepping closer towards her.

He stared intensely in her eyes. He missed her more than he knew. Seeing her did something to him. But knowing she was harboring something deep inside that was slowly eating at her was scary. He knew inner pain. He nursed wounds from the time he was six years old. There was always a disappointment. Always a hurdle. Emotional devastation became a way of life. He navigated through it and it was why he could see Calista so clearly.

"Me! No, it's that girl. What's her name? Keisha… You didn't say anything about having no kids."

"I didn't have time. I was going to tell you. We hit it off so good I wanted to wait. I was scared I would lose you."

"Lose me," she said.

"Yes! You think I didn't notice you were out of my league. All those degrees. All that accomplishment. You have a law degree Cali. You're a fucking lawyer."

"I'm not. I just got the degree. I don't practice."

"Why not?" he asked.

"I don't know why not ok."

"You do know. You see…All these secrets. All this rebellious shit you doing like you got it out for someone and the only person you're hurting, is you."

"No, you're hurting me. You leave me just like that. I'm disposable to you. One bad moment and I get tossed aside. You're the only one hurting me," she said, her voice filled with emotion as she tried to walk around him so she could get to her car. KC grabbed her. He pulled her close and held her face.

"I don't want to let you go. I miss you. But from now on…Someone asks if I'm you man, the answer is *yes*. That shit hurt when you told your sister and your parents that we were just friends. No more of that shit. You got that?"

"Yes," she replied, moving into his chest and burying her face on him. KC rubbed her hair and comforted her. He was certain she needed something to help get out of her own way. He had a solution. Therapy with his sister's therapist. A woman he went to see a few times. She was remarkable. He hoped Calista would agree.

Chapter Six

Not As It Seems

Rohan walked through the building headed to his office. He saw the son of one of the church members approaching. Rohan had put in a good word and got the young man hired.

"Congressman Jeffries," the man greeted.

"Harlan…,"

"Sir I wanted to talk to you about something."

"Ok. I have a minute," Rohan replied, stopping mid-stride.

"Oh… um…I meant when you had a moment."

"This is the only moment I have Harlan. Speak," Rohan said, his voice going up an octave.

Harlan instantly felt nervous. Rohan was intimidating enough without using his voice in a harsh manner. He looked like a man one shouldn't play with and now Harlan regretted stepping to him. But he was here. He had gotten the man's attention. And so now, he would need to finish what he started.

"I wanted to ask if I could court your daughter sir."

"What…"

"I um…I like Avery sir. We've been talking on the phone. She said you wouldn't approve and so I wanted to talk to you about it."

"She said that. Hmphh," Rohan replied, his mood taking on something Harlan did not understand. He couldn't tell if Rohan was pissed or just thrown through a loop.

"Avery is in college, young man. She has no room or time for a relationship. Do not disrupt what she has going.

You understand me," Rohan said with tension thick enough to cut.

"Sir..."

"Do I need to repeat myself. I am asking you to back off and allow her to finish school. If this is real it will still be there. Right?" he said.

"Yes. Yes it will sir."

"Great! Now if you'll excuse me, I have a meeting to attend. You have yourself a good day."

♦

Sophie walked across the college grounds headed back to her dorm room. She hoped Avery's class was over so the two of them could go enjoy lunch at the new Coney Island up the way.

"*Sophie, Sophie*. Remember that line from that movie The Color Purple," a fellow student said as he approached.

"Don't Sophie me. Where my shit," she said.

"I forgot your order. Did you want cookies or gummies?" the young man asked.

“Boy I want gummies. They pack a more powerful punch.”

“No, they don’t. I got some brownies that have double the dose. You will be higher than a kite. I promise you.”

“Then brownies it is. When?” she asked.

“Huh?”

“When I’m getting my shit?” she asked.

“Tonight. What about your girl. The new rich kid.”

“That’s a whole grown ass woman and she don’t get high.”

“Alright,” he said, turning and skipping towards his building. Sophie looked on for a moment then continued on. As she neared the parking lot, she noticed a black Bentley.

“Shit. What the…It’s late,” she said. She knew the presence of the car meant Avery’s parents were there, which meant she would not be getting high until they left.

Sophie approached the door and paused. An eerie silence followed by a strange sound gave her pause. Sophie stepped back. She was never fond of the Jeffries. Monica was strange and gave off fake vibes and Rohan was a whole mood. He was mean and uptight and she would rather not enter.

Sophie walked down the hall towards a friend's room and ran around the corner to hall south when she heard the door opening. She peeked and saw Rohan leaving. He looked upset which was nothing unusual. What was strange was the absence of Monica. Sophie furrowed. She watched as he walked towards the west end of the hall and exited through the stairway. It was an odd visit. Late at night and without his wife. Sophie dreaded what it could mean but she also realized it meant nothing. Their classes sometimes ended at night and so if he needed to see his daughter, and it was a day that she had classes all day, it made sense that he would visit late.

The dorm room was dark except a television and a small night lamp. Sophie could hear water running in the bathroom. Her thoughts ran wild as she tried to place the strange late night visit. She knew about men coming into their daughter's rooms at night and started looking around for any proof that something foul had occurred. The bed was made and the room seemed normal. Just as Sophie made her way around the room, Avery exited the bathroom looking normal.

There was no indication she had been accosted by her father. Sophie breathed a sigh of relief.

"Hey," Sophie greeted.

"Hey."

"I was hoping you were free to go to that new Coney Island. They had something on the menu called a Chicken Pita Melt that I hear is phenomenal. Wanna go?" she asked.

"No. I'm really tired," Avery replied.

"What did you eat today?"

"I had a corndog and fries from the cafeteria."

"Oh hell no Avery. That shit is not food. Come on. Let's get out of here," Sophie said. Just then Avery grabbed her mouth as her eye's got big.

"What's wrong?" Sophie said, as she walked to her friend.

Avery ran into their bathroom and slammed the door. Sophie could hear her vomiting. She took a step back then shook her head and turned towards her side of the room. She sat on her bed and waited. Soon the door opened slowly and Avery emerged.

"What the fuck Avery. See…I told you. That cafeteria food is no good. Just mentioning it got you sick. I wouldn't eat now, if I were you. But you can still walk with me. You probably need air."

"It's not the cafeteria food."

"What do you mean?"

"I threw up yesterday too."

"What the fuck girl. You probably pregnant."

"What!"

"Yes. That's the only thing make a girl sick on the daily. Who you been seeing? That guy Harlan you talk to every night," she said.

Avery instantly shut down. Talks of a man in her life made her jumpy. Her family could never know of Harlan. She needed Sophie to get the message fast.

"Please don't say that name. He and I are just friends. If my family found out they would cut me off. I can't be tied to him. Promise you won't say anything. My father probably has spies here. Knowing him…He has an informant planted to make sure I do what I am supposed to. I can't be tied to any man right now. I have to get straight A's and there is no room for a man. Got that?"

"Yes. Damn girl. Ok! I get it. But you're grown. Why would your parents be so concerned? You're a human. Us girls have needs. Why can't you call your own shots?"

"I do. I just don't want to disappoint them. I come from a family of educated people. They expect me to excel the way they did. I don't expect you to understand," Avery said, her expressive eyes carrying with them a seriousness Sophie had not seen.

"What is that supposed to mean?"

"You were raised by your aunt Sophie. It's not the same."

"Wow Avery. My aunt was fabulous, rest her soul. She removed me from a horrible, filthy environment. You could never begin to know what life was like for me," she said, as her eyes watered up.

"Oh Sophie I didn't mean anything by it," Avery said. Sophie turned and walked out their dorm room. She felt insulted. Avery had crossed the line with her perfect family pitch. It was too much.

Avery sat up all night waiting for Sophie to return. By three o'clock she slipped into her torn custom designed converse and headed out. She knew of a few parties going on and figured she would start there first.

Avery knocked on the door of a popular dorm room. There was light music playing in the background. The party was private and by invitation only. The unit was not supposed to throw parties so the occupants were being hush about it. After a few knocks Avery stood against the wall hoping someone showed up who was invited. Soon a man showed up and knocked three times waited then knocked three times again. He looked at Avery and simulated a kiss with his lips. She rolled her eyes as she waited for the door to open.

"What up," a young guy greeted, as Avery tried to peek inside.

"No strays. I don't know you so you can't come in," the student said.

"I don't want to come in. I am looking for someone. It's important," Avery said.

"Who?"

"Sophie Mitchell. Do you know her?" she asked.

"Of course. Who doesn't know Sophie. She's popular, if you know what I mean. And no…She aint here."

Avery furrowed at his words. She wasn't sure what he was trying to say. The only thing she was sure of was that he had just insulted her friend.

"Alright," she said, as she left.

The young man shut the door. Avery turned to leave. Suddenly the door sprung open again.

"My boy said I should let you stay. You wanna party? We pay?" he said.

"What! No!" Avery replied, turning and leaving out quickly. She didn't like the proposition. She had no sex to sell. The proposition was nothing new. Plenty of the girls was having sex in exchange for something. Avery was sheltered but it didn't go over her head. She was naïve but she was aware that men held sex in high regards. They would do anything to get it. It was the reason she kept her body from them. Rohan had warned her that men were dangerous. That she was delicate and special. Avery believed his words with every fiber of her being. She trusted her father. He was rough and controlling but he was also generous and ever present. And even though she was far away from him, his words still rang loud and clear. Men were off limits until she was much older. It was a rule she planned to follow.

"Sophie," Avery shouted, as she approached her building. Sophie was leaned against the building looking out of it. Her eyes were low and sunken. Her skin clammy and damp. She had taken something and Avery was terrified for her.

"Sophie speak to me. What is this? What did you take?" she asked. "Oh my god. I'm calling 911."

"Hello what is your emergency," the operator said.

"Please help. My friend is not responding to me. She looks spacey. Completely zoned out."

“Is she breathing?”

“Yes.”

“Can she stand?”

“Yes, but barely. She was leaning against the wall.”

“What is your location?”

“I am at Centerstone Apartments right on U of M grounds. We are at the east end dorms. Please hurry.”

“Is she diabetic?”

“Look…I don’t know. We’ve been roommates for a few months now. I don’t know a whole lot about her.”

“What did she take?”

“I don’t know!”

Suddenly a guy approached them. Avery got suspicious. He held something in his hand as he looked around like he was running from the cops. There was something sneaky in his manners. Avery held her hand up.

“Who are you?”

"Her friend. My name is Spike. I got something for her," he said, as he pushed something into her abdomen.

"What is that?" Avery shouted.

"Hang up… Now! You're going to get her in trouble. Hang up," he said. Avery shook her head no. The guy grabbed her phone and ended her call then handed her phone back.

"She'll get kicked out of school. Don't you know that. You must be the rich girl from Ohio. I'm Spike. Me and Sophie party together. Help me get her back to her dorm room before the cops come. We are not supposed to have drugs on campus or in the dorms. It's a violation. She will get sent home with the quickness. And trust me, Sophie will lose it on you for causing her to have to go home. She'll be fine. Just about another minute or so.

"Mmmm," Sophie moaned.

"See… It's called Narcan. Help me get her inside," Spike said.

"Spike! Hi baby," Sophie said with delight. She looked to her left. "Avery…My other baby. Where we going?" she asked.

"Getting you back inside. You took the whole thing. I told you to slow down. You almost OD'd," Spike said.

"Aww shit! Let me go. I'm good," Sophie said, pulling her arm from around their necks. She paused then walked slowly up the steps to the dorm entrance.

"You good from here?" Spike asked.

"Yeah nigga damn. I'm good. What the fuck was that? Don't be lacing my shit with nothing. You know I can't handle that shit."

"You took Brad shit. That wasn't your bag. I was gone for two seconds and your ass had taken his shit and bounced."

"Oh damn. Sorry. I feel sick now. Bye. I'll see you tomorrow," Sophie said.

"Just so you know…Mary Poppins called 911," he said.

"Avery!"

"What girl. You wasn't responding. I couldn't stand by and let you die. I was trying to get you help."

"Die! Girl aint nobody dying. His shit just makes you zone out. No big deal," Sophie said, as she used her key and went inside with Avery right behind her.

The women went inside their room. Avery plopped down on her bead and kept her eyes on Sophie. The brief and tense moment had her heart still pounding.

"Cut your phone off for the next twenty minutes. That operator is going to call you back. They have to make contact. It's part of their protocol. If you dial 911, they have to call back."

"Oh shit, they already did. My phone is on silent."

"See. Told you. Cut it completely off so they can't track it or nothing."

"Why you use drugs?" Avery asked bluntly.

"Why? What kind of question is that?" Sophie said. Avery was serious. Calista used them too and she didn't understand what drew the women to it.

"Long story. I told you already...My life was no picnic."

"I waited for you."

"Why? Because you insulted me earlier. No apologies. No regrets. People say what they want. You speak how you feel. That's why *sorry* is redundant," she said.

Avery felt even worse. She wanted to say she was sorry because she meant it. But Sophie's powerful words made her think. It seemed the apology would fall on deaf ears. But Avery still had questions. Sophie was a mystery of sorts. She was open but at the same time closed off. She appeared free with information but also private. Her life seemed riddled with all that her parents had warned her about. Drugs. Open doors for men. A party lifestyle. All things that were sins. Things that reduced a woman's value.

"Listen...I don't want to talk about me. What happened to me happened a long time ago. If you must know I was molested. My father and my uncle had sex with me. Told me I was a whore like my mother. Said I would never amount to anything. And here I am getting straight A's in some of the hardest classes at U of M. Proof that no one can define you. They tried to destroy me, yet I survived. They tried to use me and discard me and I'm still here. The drugs help me deal with it at times. Nothing more. I'm getting through the dark days," Sophie said.

"Damn Sophie. Did you love your father?"

"Did you hear a word I said. No, I did not. He raped me Avery."

"Raped?"

"Yes. I did not consent. Besides a young girl can't consent and a father doing it is vile and despicable. I was a child. He even lied to his girlfriend. She caught him and he said I wanted it. I would never consent to my own father touching me."

"My father said that fathers love their girls first. Before a man does."

"What! Avery! What the fuck. Have you been with your father?" she asked, her eyes wide with anticipation and fear. Avery immediately responded by shaking her head *no*.

"Yes, he did. I can tell. I see it on you Avery. You look infatuated as you talk about him. Yes, he did. That bastard!"

"No, he didn't Sophie. Oh my god. Like really! Don't say that. He would never," she replied. Sophie stood over her trying to read the look on her face. She didn't believe her. Something was off. The conversation was strange. Saying that he told her fathers love their daughters first was similar to what her father said. It was the same playbook. As if the men took a course in it.

"Fine! Let's just drop it. If you're not going to be honest," Sophie said.

"I am. My father is the best. I love him. He spoils me. I can go to him with anything and he will be there. More than my mom. Yes, let's just drop it."

Sophie plopped down on her bed and turned the television on. She was bothered to the point of no return. Avery didn't make sense. The women had nothing in common. But Sophie liked her. She didn't want them to fall out.

"You still throwing up?"

"No. I feel ok. I guess whatever I ate needed to come out. I've been fine since."

"Good. Sorry for what I said. I can't say anything about your father. I don't know him."

"We're good Sophie. I know you mean well. I trust you. No worries. I'm sorry too. Sometimes I talk out of pocket."

"We are good. We will always be good. One thing about me… I don't hold grudges. If ever you want to talk, I'm here. If ever you need me, I'm here. I think we're going to end up besties. One thing I noticed about you is you do show up. You came looking for me and I love that. You check on your friends."

"Thanks girl. Of course, I came looking. I know you love your sleep, and when you wasn't here, I panicked."

"Thanks. It could have gone bad. Thanks for being there."

"You're welcome."

Smokey Moment

Smokey Moment

Chapter Seven

Daddy Issues

Rohan walked through his front door exhausted. Monica was there with a Jack Daniels and Coke to help soothe his day.

"You alright baby?" she asked.

"Yeah. Just tired. What's for dinner?"

"Roast, baby potatoes, carrots and cornbread. Made a special gravy with soy sauce and rum for the roast. Simply delicious," she replied.

"You ate already?" Rohan asked, stopping and giving her his full attention. The look on his face was hard to read.

He was stressed and the question made no sense. Monica hesitated then gave him a warm smile to lighten the mood.

"Of course not. You know I don't eat without you. Come on baby. I wouldn't. What's wrong? Is there something you want to talk about?"

"No. Just prepare my plate please. I want to eat it in the room. I'm tired."

The air was thick with tension for reasons Monica could not figure. Her husband had bad days. It came with the territory. He was responsible for a lot. Pressure was on him to help write the narrative of the government's responsibility with the world around them Namely the state of Ohio. It was a lot of territory. He spoke with the Governor. With mayors. With those responsible for enforcing the laws that govern the land. Rohan was built for it. But lately he seemed ill equipped. Monica wondered if he was overwhelmed. They were wealthy enough for him to retire.

Monica wanted to wash away the stain of the day. A good massage and a glass of cognac, might do the trick. Soon the phone rang.

"Hello."

“Hey. I meant to call you back. You busy,” Monica’s sister Carla said.

“Oh my god. You are impossible. I called you this morning. You are not calling me back this late. What if it were important?”

“Then you would have called me back,” Carla chuckled.

“Yeah. But I can’t talk now. Rohan just got home.”

“Oh! It’s so late.”

“I know. His meetings sometimes run late.”

“If Thomas came home at eleven I swear…,” Carla said.

“Don’t start. Rohan works hard. He doesn’t mind pulling all-nighters.”

“All nighters. Monica…He is a congressman. There are no all-nighters. But you know him. You turn your head but I know you see through his bullshit. Tell me something…What ever happened with your housekeeper? Why did she leave so abruptly?” Carla asked.

"Why you bring that up. I don't know. It wasn't a conspiracy."

"You never asked her?"

"No! I never saw her after she left."

"And you don't think he has something to do with that?"

"No! Look…I live in a million dollar home. My life is wonderful. If it's not you, it's the women at *New Horizons Faith Everlating* saying things about what they think they see."

"Monica, that's not why I called you. I am just returning your call. Forget it. That's your life. Not my business. But what have the women at church been saying."

"Nothing!"

"What Monica," she repeated. Monica looked behind her to ensure Rohan was not close.

"Mrs. Jackie asked if I was at the Marriott a few weeks ago. Said she thought she saw Rohan walk in with some woman. She said it was our car. You know the Bentley is custom with that stripe on the side. Very distinguishable. I was not there. I've been on edge ever since. It wasn't me. Oh Carla…I think he is. I think he's…," she said, as Rohan walked in.

"I'm what?" Rohan said, as he walked in. He gave her a grimacing look as he made his way towards the refrigerator. Monica's mouth sat agape. She could see he was upset with whatever portion of her conversation he overheard.

"Um…Carla. Let me call you back. Rohan needs me," she said, hanging up abruptly. "What?" she said nervously.

"Who was that?" he asked.

"Carla. She was just returning my call. I'm fixing your plate."

"No, you were on the phone. Were you talking about me?"

"No hun. I'm heating up your plate. Go relax. I'm bringing your food."

"Hurry up. I'm hungry and I'm tired. It's late. She should call you during normal hours. You're married."

"Don't do that. She might have called late but you came home late, which is even worse. I ignored that and the fact that you come home with an attitude on top of it."

"You talk to me like that when you don't want for nothing. I didn't know you had an issue with anything. I come home in a bad mood because there is a lot on my plate. I'm trying to achieve something here. Everyone has their hand out so I can't slow down. I have responsibilities you wouldn't begin to understand. And I come home to a wife who listens to idle gossip. Someone saw me at Marriott? Did it occur to you that they have conference rooms? I have attended meetings there at least three times in the last several months. But you'd rather entertain women who want to be in your shoes."

"I'm sorry. I'm not trying to start anything. Jackie did approach me and say that. I didn't know. I did fear maybe something was going on."

"What…An affair. I have no interest in anyone other than my wife. Those women envy you. Like Pastor Jennings says…Envy breeds everything contemptable. Don't get caught up in their web. They want you to fail by making you question your life. Your vows. Because they want it. They want your spot. We are better than that. I love you. Do you want to follow them or do you want to follow your husband?" he said. Monica walked closer.

"I will always follow your lead. It's us against the world. You were my everything and still is. When we met, I couldn't wait to start my life with you. I felt lucky to have you. You could have anyone and you wanted me. I love you. I follow you and I believe in you."

Rohan touched her face and rubbed his thumb across her chin. He raised her face to look up at him. His six foot lean frame was powerful. His eyes were serious. His salt and pepper hair and smooth silky skin were mesmerizing. He radiated confidence and sex appeal, even still at his age. Monica wanted him. Her husband did it for her. The truth was she couldn't stand anything else than the reality in which she thrived in. If there was an affair going on, she would believe it when she saw it. Gossip was the work of the devil, as far as she was concerned.

There were some fears that came with women like Mrs. Jackie reporting seeing him in places that bordered on suspicious. She worried about their image. But she also worried that if there was an affair, it could produce children. Rohan was young enough to still impregnate a woman. Outside children would be the death of them. She wanted to be the only woman who bore him children. Her offspring would be the only Jeffries. The only heirs to his twenty million dollar fortune. All Monica's life, she was taught to dream big and marry rich and she'd done just that. There was no way some young hottie with perky breasts and a round ass would walk off with her hard work. Who he was, was in direct relation to who he was married to.

It was Monica who worked and helped support his way through college. He returned the favor and she was able to get through med school and even worked for a while. It was also her hard work that got him elected. It was her dream as it was his and they achieved a lot in a short time. No one would get her rewards. And no one would have his dick on the nightly. His ten inch, thick rod that still got hard as rocks belonged to her. She grabbed a few napkins and placed it on the tray. It was time to pamper her man.

"Now go on. I'm bringing your plate."

Smokey Moment

Chapter Eight

Movin Different

"You were incredible," Rohan said, as he walked up from behind and kissed his wife's neck. The fragrant aroma of Este Lauder's newest fragrance did something to him. Monica giggled like a school girl, completely aware that he could never resist certain scents. After fucking off and on for over an hour, she had awakened with a throbbing vagina and was ready for more.

"Let's go…," she said, turning around to face him before she stopped abruptly. "Wait! Where are you going? It's Saturday," she asked.

"I know. I won't be gone long. I'm going to my office to meet with a group regarding that lawsuit. That one I told you about where several business owners plan to file regarding the rezoning of their area. I won't be long," he said.

"On a Saturday Rohan…You never…," she said, before he interjected.

"I know, but everyone is so busy these days. This was the only way to get them all at once. We had to set the meeting for a weekend," he said in his watered-down Jamaican accent. He was born of Jamaican parents even though he was Brooklyn bred.

"What about the show?" she shouted.

"We'll go later if I still have time."

Monica watched as Rohan walked towards the front door. This was her life. Intense moments of passion followed by abandonment. It seemed the last year had him behaving differently. She wasn't sure what it was, but she also didn't believe he had a meeting. Whenever they made love, he found ways to part soon after. The only reason he had not parted the night before was simply because it was too late to do so.

"He's lying. No way he's going to his office," she said as she moved quickly to get dressed. She could hear the engine of his Escalade still resonating throughout the garage and the kitchen area.

The Escalade made its way down Broadway. Monica stayed a few cars back, keeping a keen eye on her husband. She had heard the whispers. Hater women from her church as well as within her own family, all told her to be careful with him. That he seemed flirty and was possibly being untrue. It was words that originally fell on deaf ears but here she was on his trail and praying she was wrong. She had part of her answer already since he was going the opposite direction of his office building.

"Where are you going?" she mumbled, turning the music off in order to clear the rambling thoughts. Rohan turned up into an apartment complex and drove down a private drive towards the end of the fancy looking units. Monica remembered them but she couldn't place who lived there. One thing she knew for certain was she had been there before. She remembered it because of the landscaping.

Beautiful small perfectly shaped shrubs that were placed perfectly along the row of units. Whoever lived there had money. The place looked like something out of Hollywood and Monica was working down her heightened senses that were at DEFCON 3.

There would be war if this was a woman's place. They were married twenty six years. They had four girls. Life was beautiful. An affair was something she would never tolerate. Not after nearly dying in childbirth for him. Not after suspecting him and catching him before, only to be told the young lady was a friend. Not after his actions somehow caused the death of her beloved husky. And certainly not after she had lived under his intense control for most of her adult life. He would die before she would turn sheepish and disappear. She prepared herself to be all in his face. If the woman crossed the line, she was prepared to turn violent. Rohan was hers. It was intolerable.

Rohan parked and got out of the car. He dusted his pants off and straightened his tie then took a few steps before stopping. Their eyes met. Monica gave an intense glare as she shook her head side to side. Rohan looked at the units then walked over to her car.

"What the fuck are you doing here Monica?" he asked.

"I should ask you that."

"No, you don't ask me shit. I told you where I had to go."

"This don't look like no office Rohan. You lied. Who lives here?"

"One of my colleagues. He asked me to pick him up. We're carpooling. I need him there and so I am picking him up to ensure that he is there."

"Sure! Let's go inside. I want to meet them."

"What?"

"You heard me Rohan. Let's go inside."

"I haven't been this upset with you in a long time. Don't bring out the bad side. I have worked hard to silence that part of me. You don't want to see that man," he said. Monica's eyes widen. It sounded like a threat and Rohan could be tough but he was gentle with her.

"See your bad side? Really. So before you take me inside, you'd rather show me this *bad side*. Then show me. I want to see it tough guy," she said, opening her car door and jumping out.

"Keep your voice down," he replied.

"No! Who the fuck is so important that you threaten me? Since when do you talk to me like that," Monica yelled. Rohan took a step back, staring at her for a moment before turning and walking back to his car. He got in and pulled off, driving past his wife slowly as he made his way back down the private road. Monica looked around. The unit looked like private entrance condominiums. They were new, upper class units that showcased an elevated lifestyle. Monica hoped the person, who he was there to see, would come out. They never did. She left after an hour.

The Escalade sat prominently at the end of their driveway with the tail end in the street. It was an odd way to park. He was definitely angry. She could tell by his awkward way of parking that was meant to upset her on sight. She loathed things out of place. It seemed he was taunting her by leaving his car that way. She was livid.

Monica pulled into the garage and jumped out. She walked hurriedly and opened the door. Rohan stood, his eyes beaming forward like a maniac, ready to engage her.

"You following me. This is where we are now. I am the man. I run this home. I earn the cost to move and go where the fuck I want. I'm not fucking around. You acting like those huzzies who look for something on they husbands because they are the ones fucking around," he said, his nostrils flaring with each word.

"Don't you dare turn this around. When a woman follows her husband, it is because she believes he is doing something. Don't you dare say women who mess around follow their husbands. Bullshit Rohan! I want to believe you. I want to feel comfortable in my skin. But no matter where I turn, I can't escape the fact that something doesn't seem right. What am I missing Rohan. I know that apartment complex. It finally came to me. Suki lives there. Janine's friend. I remember you sitting and talking with her at Janine's party. Is something going on. I'm waiting for Janine to return my call so I can see which unit Suki lives in. You got out near number 1150. I swear if you've started an affair with her, I will burn you. I will take everything!"

"I'm not fucking that girl. Listen to yourself. And you won't take everything. It won't play out that way."

"Excuse me."

"You heard me. Try me Monica. Just try me. I will destroy it all before I give you one dime. You think you're going to take half my money because you're coming unglued. Get yourself together. Maybe you should start back on those meds Dr. Weinstein had you on."

"That was twenty years ago. Fuck you. You don't carpool. All you've been doing lately is lying to me. You better hope your shit stays hidden. I know your fucking someone," she said, walking away from him.

She jogged up the stairs, the sound of sniffles making it clear she was breaking down. Rohan sighed as the sound of a slammed door resonated. He looked off. His mind raced a mile a minute. Losing the love, attention and respect of the only woman who ever cheered his every move would be difficult. He did love her. He did not want her to know the truth. That he was a sex addiction. That he had a problem that he hoped to get a handle of. He loved the power. He loved the attention. His position coupled with his money parlayed him into a position of dominance over many of the women around him. Even his daughters.

"Hey," he said, as he walked into their room. Monica kept her eyes on the television as she clutched a Kleenex tightly. Rohan approached with caution. He hadn't seen Monica that mad. He hadn't seen tears that were related to something he'd done, in years. She was solid. Strong. Resilient. It took a lot to get her worked up. She was trusting to a fault. Something he abused as he kept a firm grip on her. Now he was losing the foundation. He needed to turn things around. He wasn't ready to lose her.

"You think I'm seeing someone. Come on. Let's go talk to Suki. You believe I've started something. I didn't. But I'll make a fool of myself to take those tears away."

"Go away Rohan. I don't want to talk about it right now. I have a headache. I feel sick. Just please…I can't go through this with you."

"So you accuse me and now won't let me disprove it. Woman what do you want from me that I don't give you. You have me. I'm home every night. I provide for you. You have total freedom to do as you please. What else Monica. Tell me what you want," he said, his eyes fixed on the prize. Monica turned her head. She stared intensely at him.

"I want you to stop whatever you are doing. Just stop. Come home at a decent hour. Stop bullying our daughters. Stop giving people a reason to whisper about you. I want the man I married. Not this new, wealthy, ladies' man who wants to pretend he's single. Because if you want to be single, I will let you be single. Don't you dare break my heart after twenty six years," she said.

"Nothing is happening. I am not some ladies' man. Far from it. What can I do to keep you from listening to the ramblings of single and married unhappy women?" he asked.

"Live a god-fearing and trustworthy life. Come home at a decent hour. Be kind to our children. Be good to me Rohan…That is all I ask."

Rohan rubbed her leg and slowly moved his hand up to her thigh. Monica kept her eyes on the television even as his touch felt soothing. She hated being mad. She hated being skeptical of him. This was not their life. They were the quintessential couple. She was a fighter. And she was again prepared to fight for him.

Smokey Moment

Monica sat up and pulled him on top of her. It was the peace offering Rohan hoped would happen. Monica made up using sex. So did he. It was the one thing they had in common. The fact that she grabbed him and was initiating intimacy meant he was cleared. But he didn't dare doubt her threats.

He needed to slow down. Remove the things that threatened his life at home. Monica could destroy him. A nasty divorce with headlines that read: *Congressman Entangled in Nasty Divorce Proceedings*, could hurt his future chances of running for office. The presidential office would be out of the question. It wasn't worth the risk. A happy wife equaled a happy life.

Wednesday church service saw a new face. Rohan typically attended service on Sunday only, and was usually accompanied by his wife. The Wednesday service was for the most devout. Among them sat a lonely Rohan who looked like a man who had sins that needed to be washed away. Pastor Jennings smiled at him as he delivered the eulogy. In the words, were powerful metaphors and mention of sin that unless washed away through prayer, could destroy a man's soul. Rohan nodded as the pastor spoke with determination. His voice loud and powerful.

As the collection plate made its way through the aisles, Rohan pulled a huge bundle of twenties and several hundred dollar bills and placed it inside. The pastor nodded with affirming pleasure. He was one of their most generous members. An ever-growing wealth and his high ranking position made him untouchable.

Looks and whispers came with such men. What no one knew was the why. Pastor Jennings knew there had to be a reason for the pop up visit. Rohan was much too busy and it was a first. He knew better.

"Rohan…Good to see you join us during one of our Wednesday services. Where's Monica?" the pastor said.

"With family. She sends her love. I came for service of course, but I also need to have a word with you. In private if you don't mind."

"Certainly. Let's go to my office," the pastor said.

The men walked as staring and curious eyes were locked in. Soon whispers filled the pews and halls. Pastor Jennings opened his office door and walked in. Rohan closed the door behind them. The pastor could feel something was off. Rohan was a man whose face showed what was going on inside. His expressive eyes had already told of trouble before this moment.

"So what can I do for you?"

"I need your wife to exit from my marriage. It seems she has been taking opportunities to speak to my wife about things she has no clue about. My wife and I have been at it for over a week now and its all centered around words said."

"What was said?"

"That, I can't tell you. I know that it came from Mrs. Jackie. I overheard my wife talking about it over the phone. We have not been the same since. You're a powerful man. You know what it's like to try to keep a peaceful home. Suspicion surrounds us even as we live righteously. My work and time away from home is problem enough. It's hard to maintain trust when outsiders are putting ideas in your spouse's mind. You know what I'm saying," he said.

"I do. Don't worry. It won't happen again. Consider it taken care of."

Avery sat on the edge of her bed rubbing a hole through the sheet. She stared out into the abyss then back at the *Clearblue Pregnancy Test* that showed two prominent lines. She was pregnant. It was devastating news.

"Girl…You'll never guess what I got. An invitation to the party of all parties. It's tonight. Oh my god. What will I wear? I have to be hot, baby. Hot honey. Like… all the stops. Nothing but supreme bitch vibes, Hahaha," Sophie chuckled, as she moved around the room. She came to a standstill. Avery sat in silence.

"Avery…You hear me. What's wrong?" she said, moving quickly over to Avery's bed. Her off-putting stare was concerning.

"What the fuck is this," Sophie said, picking up the Clearblue stick and looking at the results.

"Oh nooooo. No. No. No. No. No. You are not pregnant."

"Yes I am. I'm fucking pregnant. Me! My parents will pull me from school. My father will…," Avery said in a barely audible tone. Sophie felt her pain. Red, swollen eyes told the story. It was obvious that Avery knew for some time, and sat there for hours crying her eyes out. The young women had become close. Sophie could do nothing to fix this. It was one of those things that could ruin a girl.

"Ok let's think about this. I know that if you don't want it you can get rid of it."

"I can't. My mother said abortion is a sin."

"This is not the time for religion according to your mother. You have to be your own kind of Christian. This is your life. What do you want to do."

"I looked it up. I read horror stories. Even if I wanted it, I couldn't keep it. Something could be wrong."

"What! Wrong? Avery don't go talking crazy. This is not the time. We need to find a clinic and you need to take care of this. Wait! Rebecca was just pregnant."

"Who?"

"Rebecca Stanton. She can tell us where she went. You can have this taken care of. I'll be right back. Let me find out where she went."

Sophie jumped up and ran out of the dorm room. Avery laid back on the bed and placed one of her pillows over her face. It was the worst news. She imagined her mother crying and her father giving piercing glares. He would then go into a rant, which was the scariest part of it all. His rants did damage. His word choice would render her broken. She would rather stick nails in her eyes.

"Hey," Sophie said, as she entered, moving like a criminal from *America's Most Wanted.* Sophie was in full covert mode, and Avery was becoming more stressed.

"Okay so look. Rebecca said that there is a pre-med student on campus who knows how to perform abortions."

"What! Are you kidding me. Sophie! No! I can't go to some quack," Avery replied.

"Yes you can. This is a matter of life and death. A baby will change everything. Hell no. You not married. You don't even see that guy. I have not seen Harlan once. You only talk to him over the phone. If he not here for you now, he's not going to be there for you when the baby is born. He a deadbeat already. Just listen to me. We can do this. The girl charges two hundred. That's it. Two hundred. You go, get it, then rest afterwards. I'll be there. I won't abandon you. It will be our thing. Our secret."

"Damn Sophie…I don't know."

"What choice do you have. Do it and move on. Just don't even think about it. It will just stress you even more. I will go talk to her. I'll set it up for you. Trust me…This will be ok. You got this."

Chapter Nine

Gut Feeling

The Kroger aisles were filled with shoppers. Monica did her best to get in and out before the lines grew even longer. But her need to read labels and check-mark certain ingredients, had her pushing through time. Rohan would be home in a few hours. Her plan for a nice meal followed by a movie with him would not be deterred.

"Monica," a female voice said from behind.

Monica turned around and was shocked to see Mrs. Jackie from church. She wore glasses but the shades were doing a poor job of hiding the huge black eye she sported. Her smile was displaced. Someone had whaled on her like they were in a boxing match. It was a sight she'd never seen. Pastor Jennings and his wife Jacqueline were prominent and appeared happily married. This was heart breaking. There could be a logical reason for it. A fall or a motor vehicle accident could have occurred. But Monica doubted it. She saw no other signs of injury.

"How are you?" Jackie asked.

"Good. And you?"

"I'm good. Picking up dinner for tonight," Jackie replied.

"Me too. You know... I'm glad we're bumping into one another. I wanted to ask you something. Something that's been bothering me. Remember when you told me about seeing Rohan at the Marriott. Did you get a good look at the woman he was with?" she asked.

"I'm not sure what you mean?"

"Um…You saw Rohan at the Marriott one night. Late. You said he was walking inside with a woman. You…You don't remember telling me that?"

"No! It wasn't me. I… I didn't see him. No," she replied.

"Wait…What? You told me this after service a few weeks ago. I know it was you."

"No Monica. It wasn't me. You must be confused. I'm sorry. Listen…I have to go. It was nice seeing you. I must get home before the pastor. You have yourself a wonderful day"

Monica watched her walk away, completely outdone at her refusal to speak on it. Monica was perplexed. Jackie was a strong woman. Not the type to cower. It seemed someone had silenced her. She feared who. She suspected something that hurt her deeply. If Rohan had spoken to the pastor and it resulted in Jackie getting attacked, she wouldn't be able to let it go. Their troubles were theirs. Jackie had nothing to do with him walking into a hotel in the middle of the night. And getting busted came with the territory. Women talked. He had overstepped his bounds.

"Babe," Rohan called out, as he entered his home. He followed the smells to the kitchen. Monica moved smoothly between the sink and the kitchen island. Her attention planted firmly on her meal preparation.

"Hey," he said, coming up behind her and planting his head in her neck.

"Hey," she said dryly.

"Wow! Good to see you too. What's wrong?"

"You! So you went to see Pastor Jennings?"

"I what?" he said, taking a step back.

"You went to see the pastor. You told on Jackie hoping to get her in trouble, which is exactly what happened."

"What in the hell Monica!"

"Yeah! You were in trouble at home because of her, so you figured you'd return the favor. Tell me I'm lying. Say it didn't happen and I will drive to their house and we can all get to the bottom of it. Do you know what he did?"

"No… All I know is if she lies on me one more fucking time I will withdraw my support of her church."

"What! You just don't stop. You dig a hole and you keep digging. How dare you involve them on something spoken between you and I, in confidence. She is not the reason you and I had a falling out! Your dick is the reason why."

"My dick?"

"Yes…Your dick and your inability to control it. I am sick of the lies. Sick of the games. You do you, and I allowed it. I turned my head hoping you would get it out of your system. I waited. Married you, knowing you were a ladies man. Knowing you had a thing. An itch you couldn't control. No more! From now on, I ask questions. I will find the answers. You try to cut off my resources. People who talk to me. You destroyed a friendship. Thanks! Be careful Rohan. My patience is gone."

"Is dinner almost ready?"

"What?"

"I'm hungry. Not going to stand here and have this conversation. Like I said, if she oversteps and tries to drive a wedge, I will shut it down! Shut… it… down! You understand me! I will fucking bring the fury. Her husband is an ally. If he wants my money, he will keep control over his fucking wife. She wanted some dick. Yeah…You didn't know that, did you. That bitch been chasing me. She has grabbed my hand. Flirted. Said things. I kept that shit from you. So be careful who you side with."

Monica stood frozen unable to think or move. She stared at her husband as if locked into her mind unable to speak or scream out. His words changed the narrative.

"Nothing to say. Nothing at all. You keep going against me. I don't deserve this shit Monica. Not from you. We are better than this," he said, as he slowly walked away. Monica dropped her head and put her hand on her hip. She was drained. His quick-witted responses didn't change the facts. She sighed and took a moment to calm her overworked emotions. It wasn't over.

The headboard of Calista's thick, carved wood bed knock hard against the wall. She rode KC viciously, as his toes curled and his mouth hung open. He kept his eyes closed enjoying every intense moment, as Calista grunted like a wild animal. KC opened his eyes. Calista's head was dropped back as she arched her back and kept position on his cock.

"Fuck baby. You come yet?" he asked. She had been in a sex trance for longer than he cared to acknowledge. He had come once already as he waited for her to get hers. Now it seemed an hour had passed and she was still going strong.

"No baby. Wait…Almost. Ahh. Owe almost daddy. Uhhh," she moaned. Throwing her body back and forth in an effort to rub harder across his groin. KC looked down at her pussy and instantly regretted it. Her thick pubic hair was not what he was used to. There was something animalistic about it. Most women trimmed or shaved, but she sported a full bush. It was old school style. No one wore a huge bush. But there was something erotic about. Something that caused thoughts of nasty exchanges and feelings that made cum erupt like lava. She had got him worked up again. His dick wanted to keep going as his energy levels plummeted. One more look at her bush and he was back wanting to feel more.

"Yes baby. Bout to cum all in my pussy. You ready," he teased.

"Yes. Give it to me. Mhmmm. Give it to me Ro. Nowwww," she moaned.

"Who?" he said, sitting up and flipping Calista off of him.

"What the fuck KC."

"Oh now it KC. You fucking called me another nigga name."

"Oh my…Fuck it. I can't get it right. I can never get it right with you."

"Cali. Do you hear yourself. Alright. Fuck this. I'm going to make a run. I need some air."

"Fine."

"Fine. That's all you gonna say."

"Yes. You been acting funny the last few days."

"You called me some nigga name. Who the fuck is Ro?"

"I did not say that," Calista said, as her hand moved to cover her mouth in shock. She looked down, keeping her hand firmly over her mouth.

"You want to tell me what's going on?' KC asked.

Calista shook her head vigorously.

"Sit down. Sit. I got something to say," KC said, in a low tone. His voice carrying the sound of defeat. Calista sat, still covering her mouth as she closed her eyes. KC kneeled in front of her. He could see she was changing. Something had her rattled. He couldn't do the secrets anymore. Not when her behaviors were speaking to him so loud and clear.

"That tattoo on your pussy. What is that?"

"KC! I… I…Can't."

"Yes you can. Talk to me bae. What is that? Who is that for?"

"No…no. No. No KC. No," she repeated. He paused to give her time to calm herself. She was getting worked up and he needed her ready to open up.

"I'm going to ask you this just one time. If you not strong enough to answer me, then just nod. Ok?"

Calista locked in on him. Her eyes were intense in their glare. Overwhelming emotions took control. But KC had figured out things long ago. It happened the night he first saw the tattoo. The one she thought her large pubic hair was covering. Because of where it was, it was initially hard to see. As KC pushed her legs back prepared to feast on her pussy, he noticed the ink and moved the hairs out the way. The message was clear. Now he just needed her to say it. Confirm his suspicions.

"That tattoo…Is that for him?" he asked. Calista allowed her pain to show. There was no wiping tears that felt cleansing.

"Yes."

KC sighed loudly. He looked down. It hurt to know she was abused. It was the worst he'd seen. She had been branded in an area meant to cause issues. A place that would send a clear message. The question he wanted to know was did she do it on her own or was it him.

"Did you do that? Did you seek that out and get that done?"

"No."

"Damn baby. Damn! Fuck. This is," he said, as he stood and rubbed his facial hair. KC was unsure how to feel.

"Is it still going on now?"

"Not now. Not since you."

KC dropped to his knees and grabbed her hands. He wanted her. He was in it for more than sex. He was with her for more than a good time. This was devastating news but the only way to help her was to stay and protect her. If his presence kept him at bay, he would stay until she said leave.

"I want to kill him but I know that despite what he's doing, you still love him. But I'm not going nowhere. You here me. I'm here. I will protect you. And we will go to counseling. Get you what you need. I need you right. You hear me. You my heart Cali. This can't happen. Let's fix this and move on."

"Ok."

"Ok? You promise we'll go talk to someone."

"Yes."

"You trust me?"

"Yes."

"Good cause I love you. That shit aint happening no more. Period."

Calista got down on the floor and laid into him. She closed her eyes as her body relaxed. KC rubbed her back as he fought back anger that could end a man's life. It all made sense now. It was shocking. He had answers. Calista wasn't crazy. She wasn't weird. She was a victim. The worst kind. Getting her help was his next step.

Chapter Ten

Unsettled

"Coming!" Carla shouted. Whoever the unannounced visitor at her door was, they had better have a good reason for knocking so hard the neighbors were probably on alert.

"Monica! What in the world," Carla said. Monica shot past her. Her emotion filled face looked familiar. Monica had come calling before, but never in such a tempestuous manner.

“I’m losing it. I am. I swear…He is playing mind games. He is. I know it,” she ranted, as she paced. Carla shut her door. She hadn’t seen her sister so riled up.

“Sit. I have scotch. I have wine. Which one, cause for sure, you could use a drink.”

“Scotch.”

“Scotch. Wow! Ok,” Carla said, as she walked to the bar of her modest two story home in the middle of Cincinnati.

“Here. Now start from the beginning,” Carla said.

“A few weeks back I followed him. He went to Janine’s friend Suki’s apartment. When he spotted my car, he wouldn’t go in. He tried to turn the tables on me. Never named who he was going to see. Said some crap about carpooling with people from his office. Blamed it on some meeting like he always does. This is all around the same time he was spotted with some mystery woman, walking inside the Marriott. The fucking Marriott,” she said, taking a swig of the smooth liquor. She closed her eyes then asked for another shot.

Carla stood and walked back to her bar. She was not shocked by the revelation. Rohan was never her favorite person and although he was destined for fame and fortune, she always thought her sister was too good for him.

"So what now Monica. You knew how he was. You wanted him so bad when you guys met. He always had the upper hand and he knew it. He knew he had you wrapped around his finger and now his dirty deeds have been rearing like a sunken body floating to the surface. What will you do?" she asked.

"I'm going to go talk to Suki. If I tell Janine she will discourage me. This has nothing to do with her. I don't want my daughter involved. I just want to talk to Suki and see if she will admit anything."

"That's exactly what you should do. Go now. Don't wait. Don't ask anyone opinion. Just go."

A cool breeze blew giving Monica a freshened feeling. Her internal temperature had risen a few degrees, on the heels of anger over what she considered an irresponsible man's life choices. There was no one to blame. Suki was a twenty seven year old, biracial woman of black and Asian lineage. If Rohan had seduced her with promises of riches, marriage or whatever had her risking a good friendship, she would need to speak on it. Monica was not there to play games. She wasn't there to hurt or attack. She simply came for answers.

"Yes," a voice sounded from an intercom.

"Hi Suki. It's Janine's mom. Need to talk to for a minute," she said.

"Oh hi. One second," her cheerful reply echoed. Monica was immediately taken aback. If there was an affair, why was she so happy and cheerful about the visit. Monica had only been there twice before and both times was with Janine. It was not the normal response of someone guilty.

"Hi. Come in," Suki said. Her unit was on the second floor. Monica looked up the stairs. She could hear the laughter of two children playing. Suki furrowed. Monica wasn't saying much.

"Mrs. Jeffries. Everything ok?" Suki asked.

"Yes. I um…I have something to ask you. It's gonna sound weird, or maybe not. I am not here to confront you. I just want to know why my husband came here a few weeks ago?"

Suki narrowed her gaze.

"Came here? To my apartment?" she asked.

"Yes. I know the date because it was one of the worst days of my life. He was here on May twenty fourth."

"May twenty fourth. I wasn't here. I was out of town. Janine had keys to my place. I asked her to check up on it for me. Maybe he was coming to check on Janine," she said. Monica looked off.

"Janine?"

"Yes. That's the only thing I can think of. Not me. I barely know Mr. Jeffries. He has no reason to visit me. Sorry…Did something happen?" she asked.

"No. Nothing at all."

"Or maybe he knows the family in the lower unit. I really have no idea."

The visit eased her worries. She was glad to know that her husband had not become involved with Janine's lifelong friend. But the question still remained. He acted strangely that day. As if he was caught with his hand in the cookie jar. Monica was going back home. If he was doing something, it would rear its ugly head and she would be ready to slay the beast.

A month went by as Rohan came and went as if nothing had occurred. Monica tried to move on as her insides felt as though she had been put through a meat grinder. The stress of not knowing was doing something horrific to her body and mind.

She loved Rohan so much it hurt. Some people settled after so many years of marriage. It was something that came with the territory. Several decades of marriage could be rewarding but it could also be stale. Not that stale was a bad thing. It was the sediment of what years of hard work and commitment produced. Two people knowing each other so well they could finish each other's sentences.

But somehow her and Rohan's book was still unfinished. What they had did not settle into some predictable romance. Her husband kept her on her toes. Something she used to fancy, but not anymore. She realized that there was something wrong in never being able to relax. Never being able to sit it out and grow in love. She felt she was still chasing him. Still trying to prove herself worthy of carrying his last name. This day was no different than the one before. She was still going through the motions as her restless spirit gave her another warning sign.

"Mhmm," Monica grunted, as she awakened to an empty bed. Rohan had fucked her several times throughout the night and still awoke with enough energy to start his day. She heard her phone buzz and reached for it.

"Sophie," she said, looking off then dialing Avery's roommate back.

"Hello," Sophie answered.

"Yes."

"Mrs. Jeffries. Avery is in the hospital. She's here at U of M Hospital. She didn't want me to call you but I can't not call. Anything could happen and I would never forgive myself."

"Oh my god. I'm on my way. What's wrong with her?" Monica asked, jumping up and running into her closet.

“I’m…I’m not sure. She seems ok.”

“Oh my goodness. Not my baby. I’ll be there as quickly as I can get there.”

Monica called Rohan’s phone repeatedly. She switched between his direct phone in his office, and his cell phone. After many attempts, she decided to call his secretary.

“Mr. Jeffries office,” the woman greeted.

“Good morning Georgia. Is my husband in?”

“He left with Carlos and Stephen. They have a meeting with the Governor,” she said.

“I need him now. I need you to find him and tell him to call me. It is a family emergency. Please!”

“Sure! I will call the governors office. I will call you back once I know something.”

“Thank you so much,” Monica replied. She hung up and wiped tears as her worries increased. The thought of Avery being in the hospital was scary. It was hard letting her youngest go. It hadn’t been six month and already, something was wrong.

"Please let her be ok. In the name of Jesus, I pray that my child is fine. Please," she prayed.

"Hi I'm looking for my daughter. Avery Jeffries," she said to the clerk.

"Let's see…Yes. She is here," the woman said, handing her a visitor's pass.

The halls towards the elevator were bright and inviting. The hospital's entry foyer looked more like a luxury hotel than a hospital. Monica walked the hall to the elevator and took it up to the third floor. She stepped out and saw a group of young girls. Sophie stepped from behind them and walked towards Monica.

"I'll see you later Sophie," one of the young women said. She looked down as she walked past, keeping her eyes on the floor. Monica didn't recognize any of the girls. Sophie was her only connection to her daughter. Avery called home less and less and didn't talk about any friends she'd made.

Monica walked past the two young women and into her daughter's room. Sophie followed her in. Monica turned to her.

"I want some time alone with my daughter. Can you girls come back later?" she said, keeping her eye on her daughter. Avery looked out the window. She had yet to acknowledge her mother's presence. Monica was puzzled by her behavior. It seemed Avery was not happy with her being there.

"Yes ma'am. I'll come back tomorrow," Sophie said. Monica followed her out.

"Can I ask you something."

"Yes."

"What happened? Why is she mad?"

"Oh um…I don't…," Sophie replied.

"Don't lie. I know you know. I need to know what I'm walking in on. What happened? The doctors are going to tell me anyway Sophie. You might as well say it," Monica said, her voice firm with an unmistakable serious tone.

"She um…she had an abortion and it went bad."

"What! Did you say abortion?"

"Yes ma'am."

"My Avery. She's been here just a few months and she has had an abortion? We don't believe in abortions. Avery was not raised that way. Oh my god. This is insane. Ok. Thanks Sophie. Um… She'll call later. Please tell your other friends not to come here. I have a problem with this."

"Yes ma'am. I'm sorry. We should have called you. We were trying to take care of it. The girl said she knew how to do them."

"What! Some girl. A student. This is insane…," Monica said, pacing and turning from Sophie.

"Bye Sophie."

Monica approached her daughter slowly. She now knew why Avery looked pissed. It was supposed to be a secret. Monica was not amused. She was mad herself. This was unacceptable.

"So now you know. Go ahead…Tell me how horrible a person I am," Avery said.

"Oh baby. You are not horrible. I wish you would have called me. Why would you hide such a thing? And why would you allow some girl your age to butcher your body. You could have died."

"I wish I would have."

"What! Avery…Don't say that. We will get past this. It's over now. You look ok. We will put this behind us and move forward. It wasn't meant. Who is the father hun?"

"God is now. I gave it back."

"Avery don't you dare. Pray and ask for forgiveness."

"No mom. My prayers never get answered. You have no idea how much I prayed. And in the end, I got pregnant."

"Who is he Avery? I want to talk to him."

"Leave it be mom."

"Leave it! So you're going to take the same route as Calista and Janine. Everybody has babies by men I haven't met. Do you girls really believe I am that much of a disciplinarian? I welcome your partners. Your boyfriends. You are not a child. If you have a boyfriend, he will be greeted and treated with respect, so long as he is not a hoodlum. No bums without a job. Sorry honey but you know what I've told you about men like that. Is he a bum and that's why you don't want to say?"

"Yes he is."

"Aw honey. Well, end it now. The child is gone and you can start fresh. You want to come home for a while? Get yourself together. You can take a semester or two off. It won't hurt your studies."

"No mom! I want to stay here. Its better for me. Please! I'm fine. Just please go. Don't tell anyone, especially dad."

"What! Your father has to know what's going on with you. We don't keep secrets from your father."

"No! Let me tell him when I'm ready."

"Ok sweetie."

"I had visitors all day. I haven't gotten any sleep."

“Ok sweetie. I will be back first thing.”

Monica pulled the door closed so her daughter could get some sleep. She walked to the nurses’ station. A man stood with a file in his hand.

“Hello. Can I help you?” he asked.

“Are you the nurse for Avery Jeffries?” she asked.

“No I’m not. But let’s see who is. Oh…It’s Marlene.”

“Can you please tell her that my daughter has requested rest. She doesn’t want to be disturbed.”

“I will. Thank you. We will only go in when it’s time for meds or if she uses her call light.”

“Great. Thank you!”

Chapter Eleven

Gut Punch

"Hold on," Sophie said, as she ran to the door. Monica smiled and walked in. Sophie became instantly nervous. She hadn't forgotten the day Monica's eyes threw darts when she told her about the abortion. Now Monica was at their form unannounced, with a fake smile and tension thick enough to cut with a knife.

"Sorry to disturb you but I came to collect Avery's things. She's home resting and we decided she's going to sit this semester out for health reasons. My husband has already spoken to her professors and everything is all set. I know she has some belongings here," Monica said as she went to her daughter's side of the room and grabbed Avery's pink and white Barbie duffle bag. She unzipped it and noticed some of Avery's personal items inside. She grabbed things from the nightstand and put then in the roomy bag. She opened the nightstand drawer and removed several items and keepsakes and put them in the bag. Monica's eyes scanned the room.

"She's coming back next month?" Sophie asked.

"Not next month. Next semester."

"Oh ok. I hope she can still be my roommate," Sophie said.

"I think she will be. Her placement is on hold. She'll be back. No worries. Is there anything in the bathroom or that closet that belongs to her? Leave any clothes for now. She has tons of clothes. Anything specific she wants I will be back to collect."

"I don't think so. She had some hair products in the bathroom. That's about it," Sophie replied.

"Can you grab them for me."

Sophie went into the bathroom and started going through the cabinets and the small closet. Monica looked inside the bag, checking to see what all Avery had. She noticed a small personal journal with drawings and etchings on the outside. Avery loved to doddle and her work was realistic and professional looking.

Monica smiled as she pulled the small notebook out of the bag. She flipped through the pages looking for whatever had the notebook pages unable to lie flat. As she went to the pages, she found polaroids snapshots. Monica's eyes widened at the explicit photo of her innocent daughter who she still believed to be a virgin.

"What in the world," she mumbled as she flipped through the pictures.

The first polaroid didn't appear to be Avery. It was someone with a lighter skin tone. Monica was in shock as the photo was of a woman's naked groin with a small tattoo near her private. Monica struggled to read the words but then tucked the picture back into the crease. She wondered what Avery was doing with a picture of a naked woman.

She didn't think her daughter liked women but the polaroids had her guessing it to be so. If Avery was taking pictures of women's vaginas, then she was certainly not into men. Monica continued on wondering what else she would find. It was another polaroid. One of a brown skinned woman with the same tattoo between her legs.

Monica narrowed her gaze. On another picture, of the same light skinned woman was someone's leg protruding. It appeared to be a male based on the muscles and hair. The man stood over the woman and took the picture from above, capturing part of himself while doing so. Monica couldn't make out the woman or the man since only body parts were in the shot. She looked off, then hurried and tucked the picture away as Sophie came out of the bathroom.

"This is everything. I guess the only things left are her clothes."

"Oh um…Yeah. Well…Um…Thanks a bunch Sophie. I should be going now. Thanks for looking out for my baby."

"You're welcome. Tell her to call me when she feels better."

"I will. She had some complications and U of M decided to keep her another week. There was an infection. She is on antibiotics now. They say she should recover fully. She should be home soon."

Monica walked with purpose to her car. Her breathing had amped up as her nerves took over. She was seeing things. She hadn't gotten over the shock of seeing naked women in her daughter's notebook before what caught her attention and nearly stopped her heart. She got in her car and held her chest and said a fast prayer.

Please Lord. Please! I'm losing my mind. I'm seeing things that aren't there. Please make this be something else. I'm wrong. Show me that I'm wrong.

Monica opened her eyes then sat in the parking lot praying and promising to live better if the thing that had her by the throat would loosen its grip. The image that couldn't be as it appeared. It was choking her to within an inch of her life and she needed to look once more. The natural sunlight would show more detail.

Monica removed the notebook and carefully opened it. She grabbed the polaroids. Four in total. She looked for the one with the brown skinned young girl and studied it.

“This is Avery. What in the world. Was someone trafficking my baby. She’s only eighteen. How old are these,” she cried. “

No! Noooo!” she cried. Monica threw the pictures then wailed as loud as a mother could wail. Her muffled cries resonated slightly. A man walking by and stopped then made his way to her.

“Ma’am are you alright?” the student asked.

“Get away from me! Get away. Go! Get away from here,” she screamed.

She leaned her head back on the headrest and gave herself time to process the pain. She opened her eyes and then looked around. Campus security had just pulled up. It seemed the man she yelled at call security anyway.

“Ma’am, can you roll the window down,” the security guard said. Monica exhaled sharply as she let her window down half way.

“We got a call about a distraught woman screaming. Are you ok?” he asked.

Monica snickered then laughed, causing the man instant concern. She appeared to be a woman coming unglued and he had no immediate answers for how to handle the situation.

"Ma'am?"

"What?"

"I asked if you were ok?"

"Yes…Yes. My child is in the hospital and I am upset. Is a woman allowed to be upset, or is that against the law now too?" she griped.

"Oh sorry. The caller was just concerned. He said you looked distressed. Sorry, but I had to check."

"Thank you, officer, but I'm ok."

The guard walked back to his patrol car and pulled off. Monica watched him carefully then grabbed the photos she slung across the seat. She gathered the pictures and looked at them again. She wanted to know what the tattoo said. And she wanted to know who the other woman was.

"Why would Avery have these. And what is this tattoo on her. Was this some sex party. Were they all together? This looks old. She's only eighteen. This can't be happening."

"Hi...Do you have magnifying glasses. I need one that can magnify something really tiny," she said.

"Yes we do. Try aisle three," the gentleman said.

The bright store offered little by way of solace. Avery and some woman had matching tattoos. Two words done in cursive font.

Monica located the magnifying glass and returned to her car. She sat in the parking lot, studying the picture. After a few minutes she dropped her hands, holding the picture and magnifying glass tight. No words could explain. No scenario would make sense. Her heart sank as she realized what the tattoos said. Life would forever change for her and her family.

"You ok," Rohan asked his wife. She had been eerily quiet most of the evening. Avery was still in the hospital and he knew that was a source of emotional stress for her. Rohan wanted touch her but he didn't dare. He was sure she was in no mood for sex. Even though he was tired, he did want to put his mouth on her and watch her response. Monica's moans and dirty talk sometimes was enough. He wanted her bad but not like this. She was in obvious distress and all he could do was allow her the time she needed to get over what had just happened.

"I'm fine. I'm really tired."

"Ok baby. Get some sleep," he said, turning over on his side.

Monica opened her eyes and stared. She was exhausted but sleep would be nearly impossible as her mind ran wild with thoughts of something vile and revolting. She needed to get to the bottom of the photos. The leg. The other woman. The matching tattoos. Something was guiding her. She prayed and it seemed forces were directing her next move. She had somewhere to be in the morning. She needed rest. A long day was coming.

"Just a minute," the voice sounded. An unfamiliar face opened the door of 1001 Longacre.

"Hi. May I help you?" the woman said.

"Hi is Jackie here?" Monica asked.

"Come in."

The woman disappeared down a hallway calling out Jackie's name. Monica heard her old friend's voice. She wasn't sure how welcome she would be, given the circumstances. A black eye was a serious thing. It was never made clear what happened but she suspected it was tied to her conversation since Jackie had been avoiding her ever since.

"Monica?"

"Hey Jackie."

"What are you doing here?"

"I needed to talk to you. Do you have a minute."

"No, actually I'm on my way out. Whatever it is will have to wait."

"Is the pastor here?" Monica asked.

"No, he's giving bible study to his elders."

"Can we talk before he returns? Maybe go somewhere safe?"

"Safe? I will be safe this time?"

"Jackie please! I'm sorry I know what happened. I know my husband ran his mouth. Rohan had no right. He talked to your husband and you suffered because of it. I can't tell you how sorry I am. I need your help. Please. This stays between me and you. You can count on that. Please Jackie."

Jackie had Monica follow her to a small coffee shop five miles from her home. She pulled up and the two got out of their cars.

"I used to come here when I needed to get away. We should be safe here," Jackie said.

A waitress sat two cups of coffee in front of them and took their small menus. The sandwich shop was unique. Books lined a book shelf for patrons who loved a good read while they sipped a cup of coffee. Jackie stirred her shot of expresso on the side into her coffee.

"Listen. I know what's its like to be married to a domineering man. Pastor Jennings is…well…a combination of sweet and sour, if you know what I mean. He can be abrasive. I have learned to work around his idiosyncrasies. But I will tell you one thing…He hadn't put his hands on me in some time. I don't know what your husband told him that lit that kind of fire under his ass, but Rohan almost got him shot that day. I love my husband but I don't do abuse. I swore I would never talk to you again. I don't want to have to kill my husband and so you and your husband had been written off. I wanted you out of my congregation but your husband is rich. Money is money. So here we are. What can I do for you Monica?" she asked.

"Let me start by apologizing again. I don't want to upset you. I'm going through something. I promise that what we talk about here will never get repeated. I just need to know something. Did you get a good look at the woman with Rohan that night at the Marriott?"

"Yes."

"If I show you some pictures, will you be able to point her out?"

"Probably. What is this about Monica? You have a picture of the woman? Is he having an affair? I mean…I didn't want to believe that. The woman was quite young. I thought for a moment it could be his secretary. But then, they looked too comfortable."

"That's what I'm trying to get to the bottom of. Was it her?" she asked, as she pushed a picture across the table.

"No."

"What about her," she said pulling back the first picture and replacing it with a new one.

"No."

"Her?" she said, pushing another picture forward. Jackie wiped her eyeglasses with the tip of her blouse and placed them on her face. She raised the photo closer and sat it back down.

"Yep. That's her. Same hairstyle and everything. Light skinned. Beautiful. Tall. And her hair was in a bun on top. Like a big ball type bun. She had very wavy hair. That's her. I'm sure of it."

"It is?"

"Yes," Jackie replied. Monica's expression changed. Jackie worried. It was not good. Whoever it was, Monica looked to be having a physical reaction to the revelation.

"I have to go. I have to drive all the way back to University of Michigan," she said, pulling a twenty from her wallet and placing it on the table.

"Will you be ok?" Jackie asked.

"Yes and no. That was my daughter you pointed out. That leaves me with more questions than answers. But thanks for taking the time. I just have one more person to see," she replied.

"Then your daughter looks like the woman. I could be wrong."

"No you were adamant that it was the person. Don't worry. I just needed you to confirm it."

"I'm sure its nothing. Why do you seem distraught? If he was with your daughter then that answers that for you. But like I said, I could be wrong. I just know the woman was light skinned and was distinct looking. Very beautiful and shapely. I saw her face and that looks like the face."

"Maybe. Look I gotta go. Talk to you later."

Monica walked hastily out the door. Jackie stood staring out the window. It was obvious that Rohan had in fact been having an affair and Monica knew who it was and wanted confirmation. It also seemed that she had a young daughter who had been violated. She prayed for her friend and also prayed that Monica kept her word and did not involve her.

Chapter Twelve

Snapped

The Jeffries home was quiet. Monica sat at the dining room table with a scotch in her hand. She was never much of a drinker but it was required. Rohan would be home shortly and she had prepared his meal and had the home spotless. It was something he'd come to expect. She put in overtime getting everything just right for him.

The walls had been wiped down. The floors. All glass was shined to perfection. Food was prepared and waiting.

Their custom, ten chair dining room table that royalty sat at before was the perfect setting. He bragged about the table that was gifted to him by a prince. Monica's life had been a dream. Pictures of her life was spread out all over the table.

One picture was of her with Janine, Roxane, and Calista as she carried Avery in her stomach. One was of Janine as a newborn, still with biofilm covering her skin and laying on Monica's stomach. Another picture showed Rohan smiling cheerfully as he pushed Calista on a swing. Nothing but memories. The better days. The days she was naïve and in love. Rohan was her hero. He told her what he wanted in life, then accomplished his goals, right before her eyes.

Monica's plate was untouched. She looked at the time. He would be home soon unless he went on another adventure. No matter what, she couldn't move from that spot. A drink in one hand and a cigarette in the other was the diversion that saved her from burning the house down. A house of horrors. A home no more.

"Bae. Where you at. I'm home," Rohan called out. She sat silent. If he followed the smell of turkey legs and cabbage, he would soon find her.

"What the hell! Pictures everywhere. You sitting here smoking? Since when do you smoke?" Rohan asked, as he slid out of his suit jacket and hung it on the back on one of the dining room chairs.

"Sit down Rohan."

"Sit down! Monica…Sit down. I just got home. I don't have time for your drama. I can see you in a mood and I'm not playing this game with you," he said, looking puzzled, wondering why Monica had not moved except to take the cigarette to her mouth.

"Hmph…*Drama*, he says. When it rains, it pours. With you it's a fucking shit storm. I asked you to sit down which means I have something on my mind. Sit," she said calmly.

Rohan pulled out a chair and sat slowly. His intense gaze had now mixed with eyes that showed his rising stress levels. Something bad was coming. His wife's energy was deep, dark and wreaked of anger. Sitting calmly in front of him, was her mask. There was another layer he had not peeled back yet. He wasn't sure he even wanted to, as his eyes scanned the old family photos.

"Tell me what's wrong? We can fix whatever this is?" he said.

"No, we can't. Aint no fixing this. Naw, no fixing this. You're like a bull in a china shop. I guess now you want us to find some glue and glue all the plates and cups back together. You can't! The damage is done! The china will still have cracks. Right? You can't just do things then make it go away. Some things are unrepairable. Damaged for life. Never to be the same. You don't get do overs on everything Rohan! Why! I just want to know why. Why Rohan! Why my girls? My precious baby girls. One by one. Did you leave even one of them intact," she said, as she paused and gathered her thoughts.

"I found the polaroid's of you with Avery and with Janine. You took Janine to the Marriott. You took… our daughter… to the fucking Marriott! You could have any woman you want Rohan. Why? I knew who you were when we met. I saw all the women throwing themselves at you. But

I believed in us. I ignored it. And I trusted you. My girls, Rohan… My girls! I want you to explain to me how my children became your sex slaves. How you stamped *Daddy's Girl* on their fucking vaginas," she yelled, her eyes in a fixed and painful gaze.

"Answer me!" she screamed, her anger growing to full scale as life felt to drain from her. What was left was an empty shell of a woman whose spirit could not take the betrayal and simply abandoned ship.

Rohan stood up. He looked like he would vomit if it weren't for his hand perched on his side. He stopped and looked out the window as he stood straighter and gathered his composure.

"They're my girls," he replied.

"Excuse me?" Monica said, rising from her chair. It was as if she had been perched on a tree watching someone else's drama unfold. But she was not part of an audience. This was her life. A drama that had her heart beating wildly. Breathing became hard. Air felt like a heavy gas and it was hard to take in.

Rohan kept his back to his wife. His eyes gazed out the window. He felt light headed. As if in a dream. This day was never supposed to happen. His daughters adored him. He had taught them how to love him. How to be obedient. How to be private in their movements. How to keep secrets. Lessons given early on. It was life as he knew it. His own parents opened the door that many western societies deemed taboo. It was nothing. A difference in lifestyle. A difference in family life.

"You heard me. Those are my girls! Mine! A woman gives the man children. Any children we had belongs to me. Your duty to me. Those girls were my reward for a life well lived. And I love them. So, don't you dare sit here in judgement of me! They love me. We are a family," he said, as he turned around. He didn't hear Monica as she walked away. He watched as the back of her disappeared down the hall.

"This is my family, gotdammit!" he shouted, as a tear rolled down the left side of his face. He wiped both eyes, wondering how deep the wound was. His mother fought the same fight, and in the end, stayed and endured. Whether or not Monica was built the same way would soon show. He hoped so.

Rohan walked down the hall. The house was too quiet. He expected a ground shaking war with words like that. This day was never supposed to be. His wife was never supposed to speak on it. Rohan felt fear for the first time. He wasn't sure what Monica was doing or what she was capable of. She had always kept her cool. No one could manage anger like Monica.

She always found ways to calm the raging seas inside. But this was a different beast. She adored her girls. Each birth was treated like some spectacular event. All new gear. Proud displays of her belly. Sonograms were taped to the refrigerator until the baby's birth. It was not a good sign that she was now so quiet.

"Monica!" he called out.

She was now being a little too quiet on the matter. He imagined her somewhere crying her eyes out. He was beside himself with anger. There would be no soothing of feelings. No comfort was coming. He didn't see how he could ease her pain when he himself felt so much rage. There was only his wrath at her insolence. She had nerve talking to him about what he considered his. And now there was a beast in him that wanted her obedience or her head.

"Monica! Monica…Those are my fucking girls. Mine. You hear me. My children! No one tells me what to do with what belongs to me," he ranted, as he walked and listened for sound that would indicate her presence. He walked into a spare lower level room. Monica stood, calm and emotionless. Nothing at all what he expected.

Something told him to leave and allow her to calm herself like she usually did. But his anger was out front and center. He wanted control back again. He wasn't leaving his home. The home he paid for. He wasn't leaving his family. The wife he loved and the girls he cherished. Rohan failed to see his actions and the consequences. Men ran their houses as they saw fit. For him, it was Monica who was in the wrong for questioning him. He was prepared to fight until the end. This was *his* family.

"What you got there," he said as he entered the room. Monica held a black shiny object in her hand.

"Oh…You going to shoot me with my own fucking gun. Give it to me Monica. You don't know shit about a gun.

Is the safety even off? Give it to me before you hurt yourself," he said, as he approached cautiously.

"You listen to me. Give me the gun. Let's talk. Let's be civil. You want out? Is this the end for you," he asked. Monica took a step back.

"Monica…Say something. Come on. You know I'm not letting you go. And the girls…What do you want me to say. I love them. I did not harm them. They love me. You couldn't possibly understand that love. Now give me the gun," he said.

"You're sick. Men don't love their daughters physically. You don't have sex with them like they are your wives. Are you insane! You love them emotionally, you sick bastard! With your heart. With your kindness. And with your protection. You were supposed to protect them from men like you. Do you see the sickness in that? The very behavior you were supposed to ensure they would be protected from, you engaged in. Those poor girls… I cannot imagine what they must of thought about me. While I was fighting to keep them happy, safe and secure…You were raping them in the middle of the night! Is that why you were always making sure I took those pills at night. Yeah…I figured it out. The pills you had that Dr. Weinstein give me. They used to cause me to sleep hard. I remember that. You fucking low life. You fucking bastard! You were knocking me out so you could have access to my girls," she said.

"That's not true. Now give me the gun," he said calmly, as he moved his hand slowly towards it. His trembling hand neared the lethal weapon he purchased years ago on a whim. Rohan took a chance. He moved quickly while the gun was not pointed at him. His hand reaching towards the barrel.

"What about Janine's girls?" she asked.

"What about them?" he said, stopping as he waited for her reply. Monica was appalled at his brushoff.

"What do you mean. I am asking if they are your grandchildren or your children?"

"That's a silly question Monica. Your being ridiculous. Now give me the gun," he shouted, as he snatched at the gun.

"You're lying. Their yours. I know they are! That's why Janine never named or produced the father. It's because it's you. I'll kill you," Monica screamed.

A tussle between two people with deep and resounding history ensued. Rohan pulled but failed to remove it from her strong grip. Monica tried to regain control over the gun. Now that she produced it, the outcome could turn out differently. If he got it and killed her, he could abuse her girls and ruin their lives for the remainder of his breaths in this world.

There was a place in hell for men like him. She wanted him to stop but she was certain he would never end it. He had done a good job of rearing them to keep his secret. Monica fought for them. This was their voice finally being heard. Silent cries in the dark as someone they trusted violated them in the worst way. A shot rang out. Monica stared into Rohan's eyes. He stared back. This was not supposed to be their story.

"911… What is your emergency?"

“I need an ambulance and cops at 1300 Fairway Drive.”

“What is the emergency?”

“Send cops and an ambulance.”

“Can you tell me what is going on there?” the operator asked.

“Hello…Hello!” the operator said then realized the call had ended. The woman glanced back at her supervisor and motioned for her to come over.

“I’m not sure if this was a crank call or not. What should I do?” the operator said to her supervisor.

“Did the caller sound serious?”

“Yes.”

“Send the cops. They can call for an ambulance if needed.”

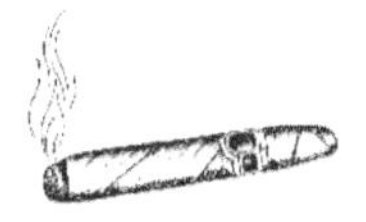

Two cops stood at 1300 Fairway Drive looking around as they knocked with purpose. The picturesque and upscale neighborhood looked like the last place a crime would be committed. Officer Watson was sure someone had either lost their cat, or had engaged in a heated argument that had now blown over. It was quiet and peaceful. Nothing looked out of place. He was sure this would be just a routine run.

The officer knocked again then looked at his partner and shrugged his shoulders. The occupants had about another minute then he would have to radio in that there was nothing at the location. Officer Watson decided to look in the window. He stepped off the porch and peered through the glass and could see a woman approaching. The sound of the doorknob turning gave way to hope and resolution. They expected it to be nothing.

“Ma’am, did you call for police?” he asked.

“Yes,” Monica said, a cigarette hanging out of her mouth.

“Ok. What seems to be the problem?”

“Come in,” the well-dressed woman said, opening her door wider to allow the cops entry. The cop looked at his partner and motioned for him to check the perimeter of the house while he took a look inside. Monica came off as unassuming and non-threatening, so he felt comfortable splitting for the time being.

“Can we leave the door open. My partner is going to have a look around.”

“Sure.”

“What’s going on?” the cop asked again.

“How long you got?” Monica said in a matter-of-fact tone.

“Huh?”

"I asked if you have time for my side of the story. I need time in order to tell you exactly what happened." she stated.

"Yes, ma'am. I have time. Tell me what happened."

"Ok," Monica said, sitting at her dining room table. She gave the cop a look and looked at the seat in front of her.

"Um…I'd rather stand until I can gage what's going on."

"Ok. You smoke?" she asked.

"No," he replied, his eyes scanning the room. He felt he was on the show *Punked*, and a camera would pop out at any moment. There was no indication of a crime. No foul odor. No blood. No smell of gunpowder. Only odd behavior from a woman with no visible signs of trauma, and who in fact looked like she was on her way to an opera.

"May I ask your name?"

"Monica Jeffries."

"Do you live alone?" he asked

"Define alone?" she said, puffing the cigarette once more, then flicking the ash in the tray.

"Is it just yourself?"

"No…I have a family."

"Ok. You want to tell me what happened now," he asked, as his partner came into the house.

"All clear," his partner said, as he joined them in the dining room.

"This is my partner Officer Johnson. I'm Officer Watson," he said.

"Hi."

"The name is Monica Jeffries," Watson said to his partner. Officer Johnson left back out. They needed to run her name and see if they got a hit. The cop considered the possibility that the woman was just a someone mentally disturbed and of considerable wealth. Maybe just eccentric. It was still unclear. But after several minutes, his partner returned and shook his head *no* indicating there was nothing on file and he was back to square one.

"Ma'am please... Tell us why you called us."

"Are there any laws for being the worst mother on the planet?" she asked.

"Um…Not really. Did something happen to one of your kids?" he asked.

"Yes."

"What?" he said, as he motioned to his partner to check the house. "Ma'am…Did something happen to your children?"

"I tried…I did. I was always there. Always involved. I attended every event. Nursed every wound. I was their when they closed their eyes to go to bed and I was there when they awoke that next morning. Three meals a day without fail. Ballet classes. Gymnastics lessons. Swimming lessons. You name it, they did it. Excelled at everything. Their father was so proud. He started taking them. I figured he just wanted to share in my joy. There is something so wonderful about watching the smile on your child's face," she said looking off as in a daze. She shook her head then continued.

"But then the smiles went away. Simply vanished. It was most noticeable on Calista. She changed. I was desperate to see my girls smile again and I tried giving them everything. I indulged their every desire. Then Calista became a problem at school. Failed every class on purpose. I knew it was done on purpose I just didn't know why. She's my smartest kid you know. Went to law school and passed the bar with flying colors. Janine was smart too. She's my most laid-back child. That girl hardly said anything. She loved her father so much. Roxanne on the other hand…That was always my problem child. That girl could be like a brick wall. No getting though her or over her. You had to walk around. Then there's my baby Avery. The sweetest kid a woman could ever ask for. Obedient to a fault. Just a people pleaser. All the signs were there. They were," she said, flicking her cigarette in the crystal ashtray, as she stared off. She looked behind her for the second cop. Her ears piped up. There would be a sound off soon. He was nearing his prize.

"George!" the cop shouted. "We have a body," he said.

"Ma'am, put your hands behind your back. You are under arrest," he said, walking to Monica and removing the cigarette from her weak grasp. Monica appeared to be in a daze. Something in her demeanor told him he was standing in a house of horrors. Something had happened that had changed a mild-mannered woman into a possible killer. He didn't have all the answers. She could have been a victim. It was hard to say, since she hadn't said much.

"You got to see this," his partner said. Officer Watson escorted Monica to the squad car. A second squad car pulled up.

"I got a possible suspect in the back of my car. Need you to watch her for a minute."

"Yep."

Officer Watson walked through Monica sprawling mansion towards the back.

"Where are you?" he called to his partner.

"Here. Last room on the left."

Officer Watson walked in on a bloody scene that looked like something straight out of a horror movie.

"What the fuck?" he said as he got a little closer. The men stood over Rohan, astounded by the brutality.

"Did she say what he did?" Johnson asked.

"No. Hadn't got that far yet. I think it's obvious whatever he did involved something of a sexual nature."

"Yeah…Damn! Why she do him like that?" Johnson said.

"Did you call it in?" Watson asked.

"Yeah."

"Did you secure the scene?"

"Yes. There's no one else in the home."

The officers left the room. Officer Johnson kept post outside the door as his partner went through the house once more. It was shocking. This was the home of wealthy people with everything going for them. He imagined their life was one filled with laughter and love at one time. Now, one sat in the back of a patrol car while the other lie sprawled out on the floor.

“Where’s Watson?” an officer entered and asked. His eyes wide with anticipation and angst.

“Fox 8 news is here. Said this is the house of Congressman Jeffries. Is that true?”

“I’ll be gotdamn. I knew he looked familiar. WATSON!” he shouted.

“What? I’m upstairs,” he replied.

“I think you need to hear this,” Officer Johnson said. Officer Watson ran down the staircase.

“What is it?”

“Guess who that is? Did you get a good look at the face?”

“No,” he replied, as he walked past his partner.

“Is that…” he asked, before Johnson interjected.

“Yep. That’s Congressman Jeffries.”

“Damn!”

Smokey Moment

Sins of the Father

Part 2

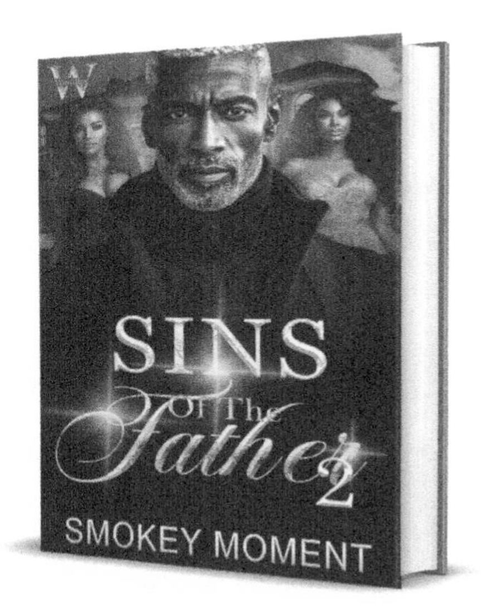

Available on Amazon

December 2023

Thank you!

Smokey Moment

Note From the Author

This fictional story highlights something that unfortunately does happen in our community. I was drawn to this story by a desire to write about something that happens every day but is not talked about. The grim reality is that children and even adults suffer at the hands of people they should be able to trust. This story is about a father, but it could be anyone. It could be a teacher. An uncle. A neighbor. And many times, the victim is left with scars that don't heal. I would like to take this moment to encourage those who have experienced something hurtful to seek help. There are free resources out there. Numbers to call where you can remain anonymous and just talk. Sometimes just talking about something will help start the healing process. Make the call if you need someone to just listen.

XOXO

Smokey Moment

If you or someone you know is suffering from abuse please call:

The National Sexual Assault Hotline at:

1 (800) 656-4673

Or if someone is in a domestic abuse situation please call for help at:

The National Domestic Abuse Hotline

1 (800) 799-7233

More Books By

Smokey Moment

Standalones

The Twin

Her Sister's Husband

Wife on Paper

For the Money

The Need to Have Him

I'm Not His Cousin

Keeping Him Quiet

Sins of the Father

That's Still My Wife

Gifted

Beauty is Sleeping

Baby Girl

The Bird in the Bayou

Hood Wife

Love Among Shadows

Smokey Moment

Two-part Sagas, Series or Trilogies:

Ways of Kings I

Ways of Kings II

Pretty Fin I & II

Stray I

Stray II New Life

Stray III Covenant

Rocks and Stones Between a Rose Series (Books 1-9)

Don't Judge Us (Books 1-3)

Please swipe to the end and leave a review of the book!

It is so appreciated!

Stay tuned for more!

Sins of the Father

Smokey Moment

For information on use of this material please contact WordRoc Publishing at the email provided. If you are an author looking for publishing services, feel free to contact us for consideration of your publishing needs. If you are a producer, promoter or screenwriter, send request to WordRoc directly.

Email us: wordroc@gmail.com

Thank you!

Made in United States
North Haven, CT
24 January 2024